American Indian
Fairy Tales

American Indian Fairy Tales

by Margaret Compton

A.W. Harrison

WITH ILLUSTRATIONS AND INTRODUCTION
BY LORENCE F. BJORKLUND

DODD, MEAD & COMPANY, New York

Author's Note

THROUGH THE courtesy of the librarian of the Smithsonian Institute, the author has had access to government reports of Indian life. Upon these and the folklore contained in the standard works of Schoolcraft, Copway, and Catlin these stories are founded.

Introduction

THE AUTHENTIC Indian legends within these pages were collected long ago, at a time before many of the tribes were confined to reservations and before the stories themselves had been "improved" by well-meaning editors. First issued in 1895, they were taken mainly from source material collected firsthand during the 1870's and 1880's by government researchers whose purpose was to record the way of life of the American Indian. These tales were recounted by the storytellers of many tribes whose camps and villages could be found on the Midwest prairies, along the Pacific Coast, in the mountains of New England, and scattered over the plains and along the rivers.

All nations and nearly every ethnic group of people have their legends, folklore, and fairy tales. The basic themes of all such stories have a remarkable similarity, and the characters differ mainly in name and by influence of geographic backgrounds and physical boundaries.

To me, it has always been a source of wonder that the American Indian, isolated by the vast oceans from other races, has in his legends so much in common with the myths of Scandinavia, the tales told in central Europe, fanciful stories from Asia and the scattered islands of the Pacific.

The characteristics of the British elves are to be found in the "little people" of the Indians; the mighty gods of the Vikings in their deeds resemble the red man's manitous. Fire, water, sky, and wind play nearly identical roles in legends of countries a world apart. The dragons of old Asia have their counterparts in America, and the humanistic behavior of animals in the stories told by primitive peoples is universal.

Perhaps in the dim long ago when the flanks of continents were joined and a land bridge united East and West, the ancestral family of all mankind sat in the shade of primeval trees and spun the original yarns from which these tales were woven and their fabric was carried across the world even to the wigwams of the American Indians.

— Lorence F. Bjorklund

Contents

The Storyteller
Himself

IAGOO, THE storyteller of the Indians, is a little, old man with a face as black as the shell of the butternut and a body like a twisted stick. His eyes are twice as large as other men's, so that when a bird flies past him he sees twice as many feathers on it, and all the little colors underneath are bright to him. His ears are twice as large as other men's, so that what seems to them but a tiny sound is to him like the roll of thunder. His legs are supple and his arms are strong, so that he can run faster and further, and can lift and carry twice as much as others.

He tells of things of which no one else ever saw the like, but the stories are pleasant to hear, and Iagoo says they are true. When the rivers and lakes are frozen so that the Indian cannot fish, and the snow has drifted many feet in thickness so that he cannot hunt, then he goes into his wigwam, cowers under his heaviest bearskin wrapper or crouches by the fire, and longs for Iagoo to appear. When the Stormfool dances about the wigwam and throws the snowflakes, hard and dry as sand, in at the doorway, then Iagoo is most likely to visit him.

He vanishes for many moons and comes back with new and wonderful tales. He has met bears with eyes of fire and claws of steel, mosquitoes whose wings were large enough for a sail for his canoe, and serpents with manes like horses.

Once he found a water lily with a leaf so broad that it made a petticoat for his wife. At another time he saw a bush so large that it took him half a day to walk round it.

As he sat in his doorway one summer evening he shot an arrow without taking direct aim. It killed a swan and twenty brace of ducks that were swimming on the river, then passed on and mortally wounded two loons on the bank, bounded back and, as it touched the water, killed an enormous fish.

He remembers when the oldest oak was an acorn. He says that he will be alive long after the white man has disappeared from the land.

These are his tales written down for the little Palefaces. They are of the fairies, the giants, the dwarfs, the witches, and the magicians of our land—America.

Snowbird and the Water Tiger

SNOWBIRD WAS the much-loved wife of Brown Bear, the brave hunter whose home was on the shore of the Great Lake. He kept the wigwam well supplied with food, and Snowbird's moccasins were the finest in the tribe, save only those of the Chief's daughters. Even those owed much of their beauty to the lovely feathers that Snowbird had given them. If you had asked her where she got the feathers she would have answered proudly, "My husband brought them from the chase."

Besides Brown Bear and his wife, there lived in the wigwam their own, dear, little papoose whom they called "Pigeon," because he was always saying, "Goo, goo"; but they hoped that he would win a nobler name some day, when he would fight the enemy, or kill some beast that was a terror to the tribe, and so take its name for his own.

They would have been a very happy family, nor would the little orphan boy whom they had adopted long before Pigeon was born have made them any trouble—he was a great help to them—but there was still another inmate, Brown Bear's mother, a wicked, old squaw, whom none of the other sons' wives would have in their wigwams. Brown Bear was her youngest son, and had always been her favorite. She was kind to him when she was not to any one else. He loved his mother and took good care of her, just as much after he brought Snowbird home to be his wife as he had done before. But the old woman was jealous. When Brown Bear brought in choice bits, such as the moose's lip and the bear's kidney, and gave them to his wife, she hated her and grumbled and mumbled to herself in the corner by the fire.

Day after day she sat thinking how she could get rid of the "intruder," as she called her daughter-in-law. She forgot how she had married the only son of a brave Chief and had gone to be the mistress of his wigwam, and he had been as kind and good to her as her son was to Snowbird.

One day when the work was all done, the old woman asked her daughter-in-law to go out to see a swing she had found near the Great Lake. It was a twisted grapevine, that hung over a high rock, but it was stout and strong, for it had been there many years and was securely fastened about the roots of two large trees. The old woman got in first

and, grasping the vine tightly, swung herself farther and farther until she was clear out over the water. "It is delightful," said she. "Just try it."

So Snowbird got into the swing. While she was enjoying the cool breeze that rose from the lake, the old woman crept behind the trees, and, as soon as the swing was in full motion and Snowbird was far out over the water, she cut the vine and let her drop down, down, down, not stopping to see what became of her.

She went home and, putting on her daughter-in-law's clothes, sat in Snowbird's place by the fire, hiding her face as much as possible, so that no one should see her wrinkles.

When Brown Bear came home he gave her the food, supposing she was his wife. She ate it greedily, paying no attention to the baby, who was crying as if his heart would break.

"Why does little Pigeon cry so?" asked the father.

"I don't know," said the old woman, "I suppose he's hungry."

She then picked up the baby, shook it soundly, and made believe to nurse it. It cried louder than ever. She boxed its ears and stuffed something into its mouth to keep it quiet.

Brown Bear thought his wife very cross; so he took his pipe and left the wigwam.

The orphan boy watched all these doings and had grown suspicious. Going to the fire he pretended to brush away the ashes. When he thought the old woman was not looking at him, he stirred the logs and made a bright flame leap up so that he could plainly see her face. He was sure there was something wrong.

"Where is Snowbird?" he asked.

"Sh—!" said the old woman, "she is by the lake, swinging." The boy said no more, but went out of the wigwam and down to the lake. There he saw the broken swing, and guessing what had happened, he went in search of Brown Bear and told him what he had discovered.

Brown Bear did not like to think any wrong of his mother, and therefore asked her no questions. Sadly he paced up and down outside the door of his wigwam. Then taking some black paint he smeared his face and body with it as a sign of mourning. When this was done he turned his long spear upside down, and pressing it into the earth, prayed for lightning, thunder, and rain, so that his wife's body might rise from the lake.

Every day he went to the lake, but saw no sign of his dear Snowbird, though the thunder rolled heavily and the lightning had split a great oak near the wigwam from the top to the base. He watched in the rain, in the sunlight, and when the great, white moon shone over the lake, but he saw nothing.

Meanwhile the orphan boy looked after little Pigeon, letting him suck the juiciest bits of meat, and bringing him milk to drink. On bright afternoons he would take the baby to the lake shore and amuse him by throwing pebbles into the water. Little Pigeon would laugh and crow and stretch out his tiny hands, then taking a pebble would try to throw it into the water himself, and, though it always dropped at his feet, he was just as well pleased.

One day as they were playing in this manner they saw a white gull rise from the center of the lake and fly toward the part of the shore where they were. When it reached them it circled above their heads, flying down close to them until little Pigeon could almost touch its great, white wings. Then, all of a sudden, it changed into a woman— Snowbird, little Pigeon's mother!

The baby crowed with delight and caught at two belts, one of leather and one of white metal, that his mother wore about her waist. She could not speak, but she took the baby in her arms, fondled it, and nursed it. The she made signs to the boy by which he understood that he was to bring the child there every day.

When Brown Bear came home that night the boy told him all that had happened.

The next afternoon when the baby cried for food the boy took him to the lake shore, Brown Bear following and hiding behind the bushes. The boy stood where he had before, close to the water's edge, and, choosing a smooth, round pebble, raised his arm slowly and with careful aim threw it far out into the lake.

Soon the gull, with the belts around its body, was seen rising from the water. It came ashore, hovered above them

16

a moment, and, as on the previous day, changed into a woman and took the child in her arms.

While she was nursing it her husband appeared. The black paint was still on his body, but he held his spear in his hand.

"Why have you not come home?" he cried, and sprang forward to embrace her.

She could not speak, but pointed to the shining belt she wore.

Brown Bear raised his spear carefully and struck a great blow at the links. They were shattered to fragments and dropped on the sands, where any one seeing them would have supposed they were pieces of a large shell.

Then Snowbird's speech returned and she told how when she fell into the lake, a water tiger seized her and twisting his tail around her waist, drew her to the bottom.

There she found a grand lodge whose walls were blue like the blue jay's back when the sun shines upon it, green like the first leaves of the maize, and golden like the bright sands on the island of the Caribs. The floor was of sand, white as the snows of winter. This was the wigwam of the Chief of the Water Tigers, whose mother was the Horned Serpent and lived with him.

The Serpent lay on a great, white shell which had knobs of copper that shone like distant campfires. But these were nothing to the red stone that sparkled on her forehead. It was covered with a thin skin like a man's eyelid, which was drawn down when she went to sleep. Her horns were very wonderful, for they were possessed of magic. When they touched a great rock the stone fell apart and there was a pathway made through it wherever the Serpent wanted to go.

There were forests in the Water Tiger's country—trees with leaves like the willow, only longer, finer, and broader; bushes and clumps of soft, dark grass.

When night came and the sun no longer shone down into the lodge and the color went out of the walls, there were fireflies—green, blue, crimson, and orange—that lighted on the bushes outside the Water Tiger's wigwam. The most beautiful of them passed inside and fluttered about the throne of the Serpent, standing guard over her while the purple snails, the day sentinels, slept.

Snowbird trembled when she saw these things and fell down in a faint before the great Horned Serpent. But the Water Tiger soothed her, for he loved her and wanted her to become his wife. This she consented to do at last, on condition that she should be allowed to go back sometimes to the lake shore to see her child.

The Water Tiger consulted his mother, who agreed to lend him a sea gull's wing which should cover his wife all over and enable her to fly to the shore. He was told, however, to fasten his tail securely about her waist, lest she should desert him when she found herself near her old home. He did so, taking care to put a leather belt around her, for fear the

18

links of white metal might hurt her delicate skin.

So she lived with the Water Tiger, kept his lodge in order, and made moccasins for the little water tigers out of beaver skin and dried fish scales. Snowbird was as happy as she could have been anywhere away from her own Brown Bear and little Pigeon.

When the old woman, Brown Bear's mother, saw them at the door of the wigwam, she leaped up and flew out of the lodge and was never seen again.

The Coyote
or Prairie Wolf

IN THE beginning, when the Karoks lived on the shores of
the Klamath River, beyond the desert of the sagebrush and
far from the Rocky Mountains, on toward the falling place
of the sun, they had many good gifts. Their forests were
noble and their deer were stately and fat. The bear was
fierce, but his flesh was sweet and life-giving, and the
Karoks grew strong by feeding upon it. But they longed
for the gift of fire. In the evening when the beautiful red
appeared in the sky they looked and looked upon it and
wished that they might catch just one spark from the fagots
in the heavens.

All the fire in the world at that time was held by two old
hags who lived at the mouth of the river and watched the
fire with jealous care. They also held the key of the dam
that kept back the shining salmon.

The Karoks hated the old women and sought for some way to deceive them, so that they might loose the salmon, but most of all they wanted the precious fire. They lay and shivered under the thick bearskin robes, for the nights were long and cold in their country, and the north wind blew in their faces and cut them sharply with his spears of ice and his arrows of snow.

They tried many times to steal the fire. Those rich in wampum offered to buy it, while some who were cunning attempted to wheedle the old hags into giving it to them, but all to no purpose. At last they thought of asking the animals to help them. But who was so cunning and so brave as to undertake the task? The bear was too clumsy and growled too much; the elk was too tall and his antlers would strike against the lodge pole of the wigwam; the dog was not wise; and the serpent was never known to do good to the Karoks or to any man.

The council sat and smoked and thought about the matter and at last decided to ask the Coyote, for he was lean and hungry and might be glad to earn some food. Moreover, he would feel proud to have the Karoks ask a favor of him, for even the meanest beast despised him because he had such hard work to get a living.

So they went to see the Coyote. His home was in the deserts half way to the mountains, where he cowered behind the sagebrush, from where he kept a sharp lookout for blood spilled by the hunter, the flesh that he threw away, or animals small and weak enough for him to be able to capture. The Coyote must forever go hungry, for when the animals were let loose upon the earth and each sprang upon its prey, the mountain sheep which was given to the Coyote dodged him, and ever since all coyotes blunder in the chase.

The Karoks found him sniffing at the ground for the hunter's trail. He felt flattered when he knew that they had come to see him, but he was far too cunning to show it. They explained their errand, but he would not promise to do anything. He took the food that they offered him— some dog's meat, buffalo steaks, and bear's kidney—delicacies that the Karoks gave to an honored guest. Then he could no longer conceal his pleasure, nor refuse to do what they asked of him.

He did not need to hunt that night, so he curled himself up snugly, put his nose under his paws, whisked his tail about to keep his feet warm, and for the first time in his life was really comfortable. He soon fell asleep, but not before he had made up his mind that it would be well to do his best for the Karoks—it was much better than hunting in the desert.

The next morning he set out early to secure help from other animals, for he could not do the thing alone. The smaller ones did not dare to refuse him, and the larger ones felt sorry for the poor creature, and were willing to be of use to him.

The Coyote stationed a Frog nearest to the camp of the Karoks, then a Squirrel, a Bat, a Bear, and a Cougar at certain measured distances, arranged in proportion to their strength and to the roughness of the road. Last of all a Karok was told to hide in the bushes near the hut where the old hags lived.

Then the Coyote walked slowly up to the door and scratched for admittance. One of the sisters went to see what was wanted and she let him in; they were surely not afraid of a miserable Coyote. He walked wearily to the center of the lodge, where he dropped down as if tired out, and shivered so that he shook the very lodge pole.

The two old hags who sat by the fire cooking salmon turned to look at him, and one of them said: "Come up near the fire if you are cold," and she made room for him directly in front of the blaze.

He dragged himself to it and lay with his head upon his paws. When he grew uncomfortably warm he gave two short barks as a signal to the man outside.

The old hags thought he barked because he enjoyed the fire. "Ha! ha!" they said, "wouldn't the Karoks like this?"

Just then there was a fearful noise of hammering and of stones striking the lodge. The old women rushed out to drive the enemy away.

Instantly the Coyote seized a half-burnt stick of wood and fled like a comet down the trail in the forest. The hags pursued him, but when he heard their shrieks he ran all the faster.

Nearer and nearer they came, until they were almost

23

upon him and his strength was fast giving out. By a great effort he flung the brand from him, just as they put out their hands to catch him.

The Cougar seized it and ran with long bounds down the winding road. The hags followed, but were no match for him and he had no trouble in handing it over to the Bear.

The Bear was very awkward and dropped it several times from his clumsy paws, so that the old women gained upon him rapidly, but the Bat seized it and flew high in the air quite unexpectedly. As for the old Bear, he rolled over against the tree exhausted.

The Bat led the hags a roundabout chase over trees, now flying high, now close to their very heads, until he nearly tired them out.

They took courage when they saw the Squirrel spring forward to catch the stick that the Bat let fall from a great height. "Surely we can catch him," they said, and they gathered their skirts about them and pursued him with furious haste.

All this time the brand was burning and it grew so hot that the Squirrel could hardly hold it. But he was a brave, little fellow and hopped and jumped steadily on through the woods, though his tail was burnt so badly that it curled up over his back and shoulders. He bears the marks of the singeing to this day.

Just when he thought he would have to drop it, he caught sight of the Frog. It was such a little piece by this time that the Frog could hardly take it from him, but he caught hold of it and ran on. The smoke blinded him and made his eyes smart, besides choking him so that he lost ground, and soon heard the hags close to him. He was the last, and only a pond lay between him and the village of the Karoks. His heart thumped against his sides and he dropped the fire in order to take breath before jumping into the water, when the old women pounced upon him.

But he was too quick for them. He dodged them, swallowed the brand, and jumped into the lake. They leaped after him, but it was of no use, for they could not swim. So he got away, and they had to turn back and go back to their hut at the mouth of the river.

The Karoks were waiting on the edge of the pond, and when the Frog crossed they welcomed him with shouts of joy. But where was the fire? He lost no time in showing them, for he spat out the sparks upon some fagots and they quickly caught fire. But the Frog lost his tail and it never grew again. Tadpoles still wear tails, but when they become full-grown frogs they cast them off, out of respect to their brave ancestor, who is king of all the animals that inhabit the bogs and marshes of the Klamath country.

After his success in getting the fire, the Coyote was a great favorite with the Karoks and dined off the choicest bits that were brought into the camp.

They were not satisfied, even now that they had roasted meat and corn, but decided to coax the Coyote to go and get the salmon. They explained to him that the big, shining fish were all in a great dam at the mouth of the river and that the old hags from whom he had stolen the fire kept the key.

The Coyote was willing, but he said, "Wait a little till my coat changes so that the hags will not know me."

So they waited till his coat grew thin and light in color, and then when he was ready, they accompanied him, with song and shouting, to the edge of the village.

He went down the Klamath River many days' journey, until he reached the mouth of the river, where he saw the old hags' lodge. He rapped at the door. They were asleep by the fire, but one of them being roused by the noise, growled, "Come in."

Instead of hanging his head, drooping his tail, and looking weary, as he had done when he went to steal the fire, the Coyote held up his head, frisked his tail and grinned at them. He was of much greater importance now, and he was sleek and round from being well-fed, so the hags did not know him.

They cooked salmon, but offered him none. He said nothing, for he was not hungry, having dined off food that the Karoks had prepared for him. "Ha!" he thought, "I shall soon have all the salmon I want from the Karoks."

The next morning he pretended to be asleep when the elder sister arose and went to get the key to the dam. She was going for salmon for breakfast. When she had left the lodge he stretched himself lazily and walked slowly toward the door. Once outside he ran after the old woman and flung himself between her feet, so that she fell down and in doing so dropped the key. He seized it, went to the dam, and unlocked it.

The green water shining with silvery salmon rushed through it so fast that it broke not only the lock, but the dam itself, and thereafter the Karoks had all the salmon that they wanted.

The Coyote grew proud over his success and was not satisfied with the kindness and honor shown to him by the Karoks. He wanted to dance through heaven. He chose a bright blue Star for a partner and called out to her night after night to dance with him. At last she grew tired of his howling; so one night she told him to go to the highest point of the cliff and she would reach down far enough for him to dance with her.

He had fine sport for a while; but as she lifted him higher and higher he began to feel cold, until his paws became numb and slipped from his partner's wrist, and he fell into the great chasm that is between the sky and the earth at the edge of the world. He went down, down, until every bit of him was lost, for Coyotes could not be permitted to dance with Stars.

How Mad Buffalo
Fought the Thunder Bird

ONCE UPON a time the Indians owned all the land around the Big Sea Water. The Good Spirit had smoked the pipe of peace at the Red-stone quarry and called all the nations to him. At his command they washed the war paint from their faces, buried their clubs and tomahawks, and made themselves pipes of red sandstone like the one that he had fashioned. They, too, smoked the peace pipe, and there was no longer war among the nations, but each dwelt by its own river and hunted only the deer, the beaver, the bear, or the bison.

In those happy days there lived on that shore of the Big Sea Water, which is directly under the hunter's star, an Indian whom all his nation trusted, for there were none like him in courage, wisdom, and prudence. From his early childhood they had looked to him to do some great deed.

He had often mastered the grizzly bear and the strong buffalo. Once he captured a buffalo ox, so large and so strong that a dozen arrows did not kill it, and from that day he was known as Mad Buffalo.

When the magic horns were needed for medicine for the people, Mad Buffalo went forth in the Moon of Flowers and by cunning, not by magic, cut them from the head of the Great Horned Serpent. For this the people loved him and he sat with the oldest and the wisest of the tribe.

Their greatest trouble in those days was the mysterious Thunder Bird, which was often seen flying through the air. It had ragged black wings, and as it moved swiftly overhead they darkened all the earth. On moonlight nights no harm came; but when it passed in the daytime, or when the Moon Princess was journeying to see her brother, the Sun Prince, and her shining lodge was hidden by the beautiful red, the Thunder Bird did evil to all who fell under its shadow.

Great curiosity existed as to its nest, but no one had dared to follow it, nor had any hunter discovered a place where it seemed likely that it could hide. Some thought it lived in a hollow tree, others that its home was in the sandstone caverns, but it had never been seen to alight.

One day in the winter, Mad Buffalo set out in search of food for his family. He had to travel to the lodge of the beavers across the Big Sea Water and far up the river. He trapped a fat beaver, slung it over his shoulder and started for home just as the full moon showed through the treetops.

While crossing the lake, when he was in sight of his own wigwam, a great shadow passed before him, shutting out all light. After it had gone he looked about him for the cause. The night was clear and the moon so bright that the hunter's star could be seen but faintly, but objects about him were as plain as in the day.

At first he saw nothing, for the Thunder Bird was directly over his head, but as it circled he caught sight of it. It made a swift movement downward, pounced upon him, and lifted him with all he had into the air.

He felt himself rising slowly till he was far above the earth, yet not so far as to prevent him seeing what was going on in the village. He could even see his own wigwam and his children in the doorway. They saw him and were terribly frightened. Their mother failed to comfort them, for they knew by heart all the dreadful tales that were told of the Thunder Bird. They themselves had seen the beautiful birch tree, which they had often climbed, torn up by the roots and lie black and dead in the forest. And the oak tree where the warriors assembled was split to its base by this terrible creature. The yellow cedar whose boughs were used for the canoe that sailed on the Big Sea Water was scorched and blighted by the Thunder Bird.

Mad Buffalo's heart did not fail him. He grasped his spear firmly and waited for his chance to do battle with the

31

monster. Faster and faster they went toward the north, straight across the Big Sea Water, rising higher and higher in the air.

At last they came to a great mountain where no trees grew. The top was a solid, bare, rugged rock, while the sides were formed of sharp boulders, with here and there a small patch of coarse grass and a few stunted furze bushes. In a cleft of the highest rock overhanging the water was the nest of the Thunder Bird. It was made of the tendons of human beings, woven with their scalp locks and the feathers they had worn when living.

Still Mad Buffalo was not afraid. As the bird neared its home it croaked and muttered, and the sound was echoed and re-echoed till the noise was deafening. Worse than this, the creature tried to dash him against the rock, driving him toward it with its wings; and when these struck him his flesh stung and smarted as if touched by coals of fire.

By violently wrenching himself and balancing his spear, he managed to escape uninjured. At length with one powerful blow the bird drove him into its nest. It then flew away.

Mad Buffalo was stunned, but only for a moment. On coming to himself he heard a low crackling noise of thunder and found that he was left to the mercy of a brood of wild, hungry, young thunder birds, for whose food he had probably been brought. They began at once to pick at his head, uttering croaks like the old bird, only not so loud; but as they were many the sound was, if possible, more dreadful.

32

Seeing that they were young birds, Mad Buffalo supposed they would be helpless, and when the old bird was out of sight he ventured to fight them. Raising himself as well as he could, he struck at one with his spear. Thereupon they all set upon him, beating him with their wings and blinking at him with their long, narrow, blood-red eyes, from which darted flashes of lightning that scorched his hands and face. In spite of the pain he fought bravely; though, when they struck him with their sharp wings, it was like the prick of a poisoned arrow or the sting of a serpent.

One by one their strength failed them and they were beaten down into the nest. Mad Buffalo took hold of the largest and strongest, wrung its neck and threw it over the precipice. On seeing this the others crept close together and did not attempt to touch him again.

He seized another, pulled out its heart, threw the body parts away and spread the skin over the edge of the nest to dry. Then filling his pipe from a pouch of wolf skin suspended from his belt, he sat down to smoke. While resting he wrung the necks of the other birds and threw them into the Big Sea Water, saving only their hearts and claws.

When he had killed them all he took four short whiffs at his pipe, pointing as he did so to the kingdoms of the four winds, and asking them for assistance. Then he got inside the dry skin, fastened it round him with the claws he had saved, put the hearts of the young birds on his spear, and started to roll down the side of the mountain.

34

As he tumbled from rock to rock the feathers of the skin flashed like fire-insects. When he was about half way down he straightened himself out and, lifting the wings with his arms, found that he could fly. He moved slowly at first, but was soon used to the motion and went as fast as the great bird could have done.

He crossed the Big Sea Water and winged his way over the forest until he came to the place from which he had been taken ten days before. There he alighted, tore off the bird's skin, and started homeward.

His wife and children could hardly believe that it was he; for they supposed the young thunder birds had long ago picked his bones. He broiled the hearts of the birds, which crackled and hissed so that they could be heard a mile from the wigwam, but the meat was juicy and tender.

The old bird was never seen again in that part of the country. Hunters who came from the Rocky Mountains say that it built a nest on the highest peak, where it raised another brood that sometimes came down toward the earth, despoiling the forests and the grain fields. But they flew higher than formerly, and from the day that Mad Buffalo fought them they never interfered with men. Their nest henceforth was made of the bones of the mountain goat and the hair of his beard.

Now when Indian children hear the fire crackling they say it is the hearts of the young thunder birds; for all their nations know of the brave deed of Mad Buffalo.

The Red
Swan

A GREAT chief, Red Thunder, was traveling with his wife
and three children to a council of the nations. When they
were near the place appointed for the meeting, one of the
children saw a beautiful white bird winging its way high
in the air. He pointed upward, clapping his hands with
delight, for it was flying swiftly toward the earth and the
sun was shining on its broad back and wings.

While the smile was on their faces the bird suddenly
appeared above them, and in a moment struck their mother
to the earth, driving her into the ground so that no portion
of her body remained. The force of the blow was so great
that the bird itself was broken in pieces and its plumes were
scattered far and wide. The Indians assembled at the council rushed forth eagerly to secure them; for a white feather

is not easily procured and is highly prized in time of war.

Red Thunder stood speechless in his great agony. Then taking his little ones with him he fled into the forest, and no man ever saw him again. He built himself a lodge and never passed far from its doorway. When Winter shook his white locks and covered the land with snow, Red Thunder fell, shot by an unseen arrow.

Thus the three boys were left alone. Even the eldest was not large enough or strong enough to bring home much food, and all that they could do was to set snares for rabbits. The animals were sorry for them and took them in charge. The squirrels dropped nuts at their doorway, and a great brown bear kept guard over them at night. They were too young to remember much of their parents, and they were brave boys, who tried their best to learn how to hunt and fish. The eldest soon became skillful and he taught his brothers.

When they were all able to take care of themselves, the eldest wanted to leave them and go to see the world, to find other lodges and bring home wives for each of them. The younger ones would not hear of this, and said that they had gone along so far without strangers, and they could still do without them. So they continued to live together and no more was said about any of them leaving.

One day they wanted new quivers for their arrows. One made his of otter, another chose sheep, and a third took wolf skin. Then they thought it well to make new arrows. They made many, some being of oak and a few, very precious, of the thigh bone of the buck. It took them much longer to fashion the heads of flint and sandstone, but at last all were finished, and they were ready for a grand hunt. They laid wagers with one another as to who should come in first with game, each one agreeing to kill only the animal he was in the habit of taking, and not to meddle with what he knew belonged to his brother.

The youngest, named Deep Voice, had not gone far when he met a black bear, which according to the agreement he was not to kill. But the animal was so close to him that he could not refrain from taking aim. The bear fell dead at his feet. His scruples were gone then, so he began skinning it.

Soon his eyes troubled him and he rubbed them with his bloody hands, when, on looking up, everything appeared red. He went to the brook and washed his hands and face, but the same red hue was still on the trees, the ground, and even on the skin of the black bear. He heard a strange noise, and leaving the animal partly skinned, went to see where it came from.

By following the sound he came to the shore of a great lake, where he saw a beautiful swan swimming. Its feathers were not like those of any other swan he had ever seen, for they were a brilliant scarlet and glistened in the sun.

He drew one of his arrows and fired at it, but the arrow fell short of its mark. He shot again and again until his quiver was empty. Still the swan remained dipping its long

38

neck into the water, seemingly ignorant of the hunter's presence.

Then he remembered that three magic arrows which had belonged to his father were in the wigwam. At any other time he would not have thought of meddling with them, but he was determined to secure this beautiful bird. He ran quickly to the lodge, brought the arrows, and fired them. The first went very near the bird, but did not strike it. The second also fell harmless in the water. The third struck the swan in the neck, but she rose immediately and flew toward the setting sun.

Deep Voice was disappointed, and knowing that his brothers would be angry about the loss of the arrows, he rushed into the water and secured the first two, but found that the third had been carried off by the red swan.

He thought that as the bird was wounded it could not fly far, so, placing the magic arrows in his quiver, he ran on to overtake it. Over hills and prairies, through the forests and out on the plain he went, till at last it grew dark and he lost sight of the swan.

On coming out of the forest he heard voices in the distance, and knew that people could not be far off. He looked about and saw a large town on a distant hill and heard the watchman, an old owl, call out, "We are visited," to which the people answered with a loud "Hallo!"

Deep Voice approached the watchman and told him that he came for no evil purpose, but merely to ask for shelter.

39

The owl said nothing, but led him to the lodge of the Chief, and told him to enter.

"Come in, come in," said the Chief. "Sit there," he added, as the young man appeared.

He was given food to eat and only few questions were asked him.

By and by the Chief, who had been watching him closely, said, "Daughter, take our son-in-law's moccasins, and if they need mending, do it for him."

Deep Voice was much astonished to find himself married at such short notice, but made up his mind to let one of his brothers have her for his wife. She was not good-looking and she proved herself bad-tempered by snatching the moccasins in such a surly manner that Deep Voice ran after her, took them from her, and hung them up himself.

Being very tired he soon fell asleep. Early next morning he said to the girl: "Which way did the red swan go?"

"Do you think you can catch it?" she said, and turned angrily away.

"Yes," he answered.

"Foolishness!" said the girl, but as he persisted, she went to the door and showed him the direction in which the bird had flown.

It was still dark, and as the road was strange to him he traveled slowly. When daylight came he started to run and ran all day as fast as he could. Toward night he was almost exhausted and was glad to find himself near another village, where he might be able to rest.

This village also had an owl for a watchman, a large, gray bird, who saw him at a distance and called to those in the camp, "Tu-who! we are visited."

Deep Voice was shown to the lodge of the Chief and treated exactly as on the first night. This time the Chief's daughter was beautiful and gentle in her ways. "She shall be for my elder brother," thought the boy, "for he has always been kind to me."

He slept soundly all night and it was nearly dawn when he awoke, but he lost no time, for the Chief's daughter was ready to answer his questions at once. She told him the red swan had passed about the middle of the previous afternoon, showed him the exact course it took, and pointed out the shortest road to the prairie.

He went slowly until sunrise and then ran as before. He was a swift runner, for he could shoot an arrow and then pass it in its flight so that it would fall behind him. He did this many times on the second day, for it helped him to travel faster. Toward evening, not seeing any town, he went more leisurely, thinking that he would have to travel all night.

Soon after dark he saw a glow of light in the woods, and found when he went nearer that it came from a small, low lodge. He went cautiously on and looked in at the doorway. An old man was sitting by the fire, his head bent forward on his breast.

Although Deep Voice had not made the slightest noise the old man called out, "Come in, my grandson."

The boy entered.

"Take a seat there," said the old man, pointing to a corner opposite him by the fire. "Now dry your things, for you must be tired, and I will cook supper for you. My kettle of water stands near the fire."

Deep Voice had been looking about the fireplace, but had seen no kettle. Now there appeared a small earthen pot filled with water. The old man took one grain of corn and one whortleberry, dropped them into the pot and set it where it would boil. Deep Voice was hungry and thought to himself that there was small chance of a good supper.

When the water boiled the old man took the kettle off, handed him a dish and spoon made of the same material as the pot and told him to help himself.

Deep Voice found the soup so good that he helped himself again and again until he had taken all there was. He felt ashamed, but he was still hungry.

Before he could speak, the old man said, "Eat, eat, my grandchild, help yourself," and motioned to the pot, which was immediately refilled.

Deep Voice again helped himself to all the soup and again the kettle was filled, and his hunger was satisfied. Then the pot vanished.

"My grandchild," said the old man, when Deep Voice had finished, "you have set out on a difficult journey, but you will succeed. *Only be determined*, and be prepared for whatever may happen. Tomorrow you will go on your way until the sun sets, when you will find one of my fellow-magicians. He will give you food and shelter and will tell you more than I am permitted to do. *Only be firm.* On the day beyond tomorrow you will meet still another who will tell you all you wish to know and how you are to gain your wish."

Deep Voice lay down on the buffalo skins, which were white and soft, and slept soundly, for the old man's words made him very happy.

The magician prepared his breakfast as he had done the supper, after which the boy went on his way. He found the second magician as he had been told, and was given a supper from a magic kettle, and a couch upon white buffalo robes.

The second magician did not seem so sure of the young man's success. "Many have gone this way before you," said he, "and none have ever come back. We shall see, we shall see."

This was said to try the courage of Deep Voice, but he remembered what the first magician had told him and was firm in his resolution.

After breakfast next day he ran forward quickly, for he was anxious to meet the third magician who should tell him all about the red swan. But though he ran all day he did not get to the third lodge any earlier than he had reached the others.

After a supper prepared as on the previous nights, the

43

magician said to him: "My grandchild, tomorrow night you will come to the lodge of the Red Swan. She is not a bird, but a beautiful girl, the most beautiful that ever lived. Her father is a magician and rich in wampum. This wampum is of much value, for many of the shells were brought from the Great Salt Lake, but he prizes his daughter far more than all. The Red Swan loves her father, and all her life is spent in making him comfortable. The old man has met with a misfortune, having lost his cap of wampum which used to be fastened to his scalp and was never removed, night or day. A tribe of Indians, who had heard of it, one day sent to him, saying that their Chief's daughter was very ill and that but one thing could cure her—a sight of this magic cap of wampum. The magician did not suspect the messengers, though he tried to persuade them to bring the maiden to him. They declared that she could not be moved; whereupon the old man tore off his cap, though it gave him much pain to do so, and sent it to the Chief. The story was all a pretense. When they got the cap they made fun of it and placed it on a pole for the birds to peck at, and the stranger to ridicule. The old man is not strong enough to get the cap back, but he has been told that a young warrior shall some day procure it for him. The Red Swan goes forth in the Moon of Falling Leaves to seek for this brave, and she has promised to be the wife of him who is successful. My grandchild, many have followed her and have failed, but I think you will be more favored. When

44

you are seated in the lodge of the Red Swan, the magician will ask you many things. Tell him your dreams and what your guardian spirits have done for you. Then he will ask you to recover his cap of wampum and will show you what you are to do to find and punish the wicked possessors of it."

Deep Voice was greatly pleased to hear that he might win such a beautiful wife. He leaped and ran gaily through the forest the next day, and the idea that he might fail never entered his mind. Toward evening he heard deep groans, which he believed came from the lodge of the Red Swan.

It was not long before he reached a fine wigwam, and on entering saw the magician seated in the center, holding his head with both hands and moaning with pain.

The old man prepared supper, for no one was allowed to see the Red Swan, or even to know that she was in the wigwam. But Deep Voice saw a curtain dividing the lodge, and thought that he heard a rustle of wings.

His heart did not fail him, and he answered the old man's questions patiently and truthfully. When he told his dreams, the magician shook his head, saying, "No, that is not the one, that is not it," to each, until Deep Voice thought he would not tell him any more. He was not willing, however, to give up the Red Swan, so at last he remembered a dream wholly different from the others, which he straightway told.

The magician became quite excited before he had finished his story, and exclaimed: "That's it, that's it! You

45

will cause me to live! That is what I have been waiting for a young man to say. Will you go and get my cap for me?"

"Yes," said Deep Voice, "and on the day beyond tomorrow when you hear the voice of the nighthawk, you must put your head out of the door of the lodge. You will see me coming with the cap, which I will fasten on your head before I enter. The magic food that I have eaten has given me the power to change my form, so I shall come as a nighthawk, and will give the cry to let you know that I am successful. Have ready your war club that I may seize it to strike with when I come."

Deep Voice had not known when he began speaking what he would say, but as the magician looked at him the words came. In spite of all the tales that he had heard about the young men who had gone before him, and the magician told him many that night, Deep Voice was anxious to begin his task. He rose early and went in the direction pointed out to him.

When he saw the cap at a distance he thought that no one was near it, but as he went nearer he found that those about it were as the hanging leaves in number. Knowing that he could not pass unharmed through so great a crowd, he changed himself into a hummingbird and flew close enough to the cap to examine it, but did not touch it, for fear an arrow might be aimed at him.

The cap was tied securely to a tall pole and no bird could unfasten it without his actions being noticed. Deep Voice,

therefore, changed himself into the down of a dandelion and lighted on the cap itself. He thrust his silver fingers under and between the cords, untied them, and lifted the cap slowly, for it was a great weight for so small a thing to carry.

When the crowd below saw the cap moving, and that it was being carried away, they raised a great shout and ran after it, shooting clouds of arrows as they went. The wind blew the down out of their reach; so it was soon far enough from them to be safe for Deep Voice to take the form of a bird. As a nighthawk he flew swiftly toward the magician's lodge, giving the call he had named as a signal.

The old man heard him and looked out. Deep Voice flew close to him and dropped the cap upon his head. Then changing himself into a man, he seized the war club which the magician had placed just outside the lodge, and with one powerful blow fastened the cap securely, but knocked the old man senseless. When he recovered, what was the surprise of Deep Voice to see, not the old magician who had entertained him, but a handsome young warrior who said to him, "Thank you, my *friend*, for the bravery and kindness by which you have restored my youth and strength."

He urged Deep Voice to remain in his lodge as his guest. They hunted together many days and became fast friends. At last Deep Voice wished to return to his brothers. The young magician then brought out gifts—buffalo robes and deer skin white as snow, strings and belts of wampum, as

48

much as he could carry, enough to make him a great man in any country.

During all his stay nothing had been said about the Red Swan. This day, as they were smoking their farewell pipe, the young magician said to Deep Voice: "My brother, you know the reward that was to be for him who restored my cap of wampum. I have given you riches that will be all that you will want as long as you live. I now give you the best gift of all."

At this the Red Swan appeared.

"Take her," said the magician. "She is my sister, let her be your wife!"

So Deep Voice and the Red Swan went home by the way he came, stopping at the lodges to take with them the wives for his brothers. The Red Swan far surpassed them in beauty and loveliness, and her daughters and their daughters have ever been known as the handsomest women of the tribe.

The Bended Rocks

BENDING WILLOW was the most beautiful girl in a tribe noted for its handsome women. She had many suitors, but she refused them all; for her love was given to a young warrior of a distant nation, who, she felt sure, would some day return to throw a red deer at her feet in token that he wished to marry her.

Among her suitors was a hideous old Indian, a chief who was very rich. He was scarred and wrinkled and his hair was as gray as the badger that burrows in the forest. He was cruel also, for when the young men were put to the torture to prove themselves worthy to be warriors, he devised tests more dreadful than any that the tribe had ever known. But the chief, who was rightly named No Heart, declared that he would marry Bending Willow, and, as he was powerful, her parents did not dare to refuse him. Bending Willow begged and pleaded in vain.

On the night before the day set for the marriage, she went into the woods, and throwing herself on the ground, sobbed as if her heart would break. All night she lay there, listening to the thunder of the great cataract of Niagara, which was but a woman's journey from the village. At last it suggested to her a sure means of escape.

Early in the morning before any one was stirring, she went back to her father's wigwam, took his canoe and dragged it to the edge of the river. Then stepping into it she set it adrift and it headed quickly toward the Falls. It soon reached the rapids and was tossed like a withered branch on the white-crested billows, but went on, on, swiftly and surely to the edge of the great Falls.

For a moment only, she saw the bright, green water, and then she felt herself lifted and was borne on great, white wings which held her above the rocks. The water divided and she passed into a dark cave behind the rainbow.

The spirit of Cloud and Rain had gone to her rescue and had taken her into his lodge. He was a little, old man, with a white face and hair and beard of soft, white mist, like that which rises day and night from the base of the Falls. The door of his lodge was the green wave of Niagara, and the walls were of gray rock studded with white stone flowers.

Cloud and Rain gave her a warm wrapper and seated her on a heap of ermine skins in a far corner of the lodge where

51

the dampness was shut out by a magic fire. This is the fire that runs beneath the Falls, and throws its yellow-and-green flames across the water, forming the rainbow.

He brought her fish to eat and delicate jelly made from mosses which only the water spirits can find or prepare.

When she was rested he told her that he knew her story, and if she would stay with him, he would keep her until her ugly old suitor was dead. "A great serpent," added he, "lies beneath the village, and is even now poisoning the spring from which No Heart draws all the water that he uses, and he will soon die."

Bending Willow was grateful, and said that she would gladly remain all her life in such a beautiful home and with such a kind spirit.

Cloud and Rain smiled, but he knew the heart of a young girl would turn toward her own home when it was safe for her to return. He needed no better proof of this than the questions she asked about the serpent which caused so much sickness among her people.

He told her that this serpent had lain there many years. When he once tasted human blood he could never be satisfied. He crept beneath a village and cast a black poison into the springs from which people drew water. When any one died the serpent stole out at night and drank his blood. That made him ravenous for more. So when one death occurred more followed until the serpent was gorged and went to sleep for a time.

"When you return," said Cloud and Rain, "persuade your people to move their camp. Let them come near me, and should the serpent dare to follow I will defend them."

Bending Willow stayed four months with Cloud and Rain. He taught her much magic, and showed her the herbs which would cure sickness.

One day when he came in from fishing he said to her: "No Heart is dead. This night I will throw a bridge from the foot of the waters across the Falls to the high hills. You must climb it without fear, for I will hold it firmly until you are on the land."

When the moon rose and lighted all the river, Cloud and Rain caused a gentle wind to raise the spray until it formed a great, white arch reaching from his cave to the distant hills. He led Bending Willow to the foot of this bridge of mist and helped her to climb until she was assured of her safety and could step steadily.

All the tribe welcomed her, and none was sorry that she had not married No Heart. She told them of the good spirit, Cloud and Rain, of his wonderful lodge, of his kindness, and of the many things he had taught her.

At first they would not entertain the idea of moving their village, for there were pleasant fishing grounds where they lived, and by the Falls none but spirits could catch the fish. But when strong men sickened and some of the children of the Chief died, they took down their lodge poles and sought the protection of the good spirit.

54

For a long time they lived in peace and health, but after many moons the serpent discovered their new camp and made his way there.

Cloud and Rain was soon aware of his arrival, and was very angry because the serpent dared to come so near his lodge. He took a handful of the magic fire and molded it into thunderbolts which he hurled at the monster. The first stunned him, the second wounded him severely, and the third killed him.

Cloud and Rain told them to drag the body to the rapids and hurl it into the water. It took all the women of the tribe to move it, for it was longer than the flight of twenty arrows. As it tossed upon the water, it looked as though a mountain had fallen upon the waves, and it drifted but slowly to the edge of the Great Falls. There it was drawn between the rocks and became wedged so firmly that it could not be dislodged, but coiled itself as if it had lain down to sleep. Its weight was so great that it bent the rocks, and they remain curved like a drawn bow to this day. The serpent itself was gradually washed to pieces and disappeared.

In the Moon of Flowers the young warrior whom Bending Willow loved came and cast a red deer at her feet, and they were happy ever after.

White Hawk,
the Lazy

WHITE HAWK was known as the laziest boy in the tribe. When his father set his nets, even on the coldest days in winter, he had to do it alone; for White Hawk would never help him either to carry the net or to cut the ice. He neither hunted nor fished, he took no part in the games of the young men, and he refused to wait upon his parents, until his name became a reproach.

His father and mother were deeply grieved by his conduct, for they themselves were industrious and frugal. They did not, like many of their tribe, return from the wintering grounds to feast and be idle; but built themselves a lodge in the forest, where they laid store for the future. At last they determined to try to shame White Hawk out of his laziness. So one night when he had refused to go to fetch water for them, the father said: "Ah, my son, one who is afraid to go to the river after dark will never kill the Red Head."

Now, it was the ambition of every Indian boy to kill the Red Head. Though his parents did not know it, White Hawk had always believed that he would accomplish it, and he often sat and thought of different ways in which it might be done, for he was strong, despite his laziness.

He made no answer, but went at once to bed. The next morning he asked his mother to make him some new moccasins of deer skin while he cut some arrows. He made only four, which he put into a shabby quiver and laid beside his moccasins ready to take with him in the morning.

He rose before daylight, and without waking either his father or his mother put on his moccasins, took his bow and quiver and set out, determined to kill the Red Head before he returned. He did not know which way to go, so as soon as it was light he shot an arrow into the air and followed the direction of its flight.

He traveled all day. Toward night he was tired and hungry, for he had brought no food with him and had found but a few acorns in the forest. To his surprise he saw a fat deer with an arrow in its side lying across his path.

It was the arrow he had shot that morning. He did not pull it out, but cut off as much meat as he wanted to eat and left the rest for the coyotes.

He slept in a hollow tree all night. Early the next morning he shot another arrow into the air to find out in what direction to go that day, and at night he found another deer that had been pierced by this arrow.

Thus it happened every day for four days, but as he had not withdrawn any of the arrows, on the fifth day he had none to use and so was without food. He was very hungry, for he had long since left the woods and there were no nuts or berries on the prairie.

He lay down, thinking he might as well die there as elsewhere, for he was suffering great pain from hunger. It was not long before he heard a hollow, rumbling sound that seemed to be underground.

He stood up and looking around, saw a broad, beaten path leading across the prairie. An old woman was walking along this path, thumping the ground with a stick at every step.

He went nearer and was terribly frightened, for he discovered that she was a witch, known throughout the country as "the little old woman who makes war."

She wore a mantle made entirely of women's scalps. Her staff, which was a stout, hickory stick, was ornamented with a string of toes and bills of birds of all kinds. At every stroke of the staff they fluttered and sang, each in its own fashion, and the discord was horrible.

White Hawk followed her, creeping along in the high grass so as to hide himself, until he saw her lodge, which was on the shore of the lake. She entered, took off her mantle and shook it several times. At every shake the scalps uttered loud shrieks of laughter, in which the old witch joined.

Presently she came out, and without seeming to look, walked directly up to White Hawk. She told him that she knew all about his determination to kill the Red Head, and that she would help him. "Many young men have *thought* about killing him," she said, "but you are the only one who has set out to do it."

She insisted upon his going to her lodge to spend the night, and he went, although he knew that he would not be able to sleep in such a place.

She told him to lie down, and taking out a comb, began to comb his hair, which in a few moments became long and glossy, like a woman's. She tied it with a magic hairstring, and gave him a woman's dress of fine, soft skin, a necklace, brooches of silver, and many strings of wampum. Then she painted his face red and yellow, not forgetting to put on some love-powder. Last of all she brought a silver bowl for him and slipped a blade of scented sword grass into his girdle.

She told him that the Red Head lived on an island in the center of the lake on the shore of which her own lodge was built.

In the morning White Hawk should go down to the water and begin dipping the silver bowl into the lake and drinking from it. The Indians who were with the Red Head would see him, and, supposing him to be a woman, would come over in their canoes, and each would wish to make her his wife.

He was to say, "No, I will only marry the Red Head, and he must bring his own canoe for me, for I have traveled a long way in order to be his wife."

When the Red Head received the news he would cross in his canoe and take White Hawk to the island. The witch loaded him with presents to give in the event of a marriage, in which case he was to be on the watch for an oppportunity to kill the Red Head by cutting off his head with the spear of scented sword grass.

White Hawk rose next morning, put on the woman's garments that had been given him, went down to the lake and began dipping water with the silver bowl.

Presently many canoes put out from the island. They were driven swiftly to the spot where he stood, and the men strove with one another in offers of marriage.

White Hawk acted as the witch told him a woman would under the circumstances. To all their entreaties he replied: "I have come a great way to see the Red Head, whom I am resolved to marry. If he wants me, let him come in his own canoe to take me to his wigwam."

The message was taken to the Red Head, who immediately crossed the lake in his canoe. As it neared the shore White Hawk saw that its framework was of live rattlesnakes, who thrust out their heads and hissed and rattled as he stepped into the boat. The Red Head spoke to them and they quieted down, as dogs at the word of their master.

When they landed the Red Head went straight to his wigwam and the marriage was performed. Then a feast was spread, the presents were given and White Hawk waited for his opportunity.

By and by Red Head's mother, who had been watching the bride closely, said to her husband: "That is no woman our son has married; no woman ever looked out of her eyes like that."

Her husband was very angry. White Hawk, who had overheard the conversation, jumped up and said: "I have been insulted, and by my husband's people. I cannot live here. I will return at once to my nation," and he ran out of the wigwam, followed by the guests and by the Red Head, who motioned to them to leave him.

White Hawk went down to the shore and made pretense of getting into a canoe, when the Red Head laid a hand upon him and sorrowfully begged him to wait at least a little time. He turned back and sat down, when the Red Head threw himself at his wife's feet and put his head into her lap.

White Hawk lost not a moment in drawing out the blade of sword grass and cutting off his head at a single stroke. He then plunged into the water and swam across the lake with the head in his hand.

He had scarcely reached the shore when he saw the Red Head's followers come down with torches in search of him

61

and his wife. He heard their shrieks when they found the headless body, and so he lost no time in making his way to the witch's lodge, where they would not be likely to follow him.

The witch received him with great joy. She told him that he must give her a little piece of the scalp for herself, but he might take the rest home.

He was anxious to return, so she gave him a partridge to offer the spirit of the earth, in case he should meet him on the way.

As White Hawk crossed the prairie, he heard a great rumbling and crackling sound, and the earth split and opened in front of him. He threw the partridge into the crack and it was closed immediately, so that he passed over it in safety.

On reaching home he found that his parents had fasted and mourned for him as dead, for he had been gone a year. Many young men had come to them and had said, "See, I am your son," until when White Hawk did return they would not even look at him.

He threw himself at their feet and told them that he had killed the Red Head. They paid no attention to him, and the young men of the tribe to whom he repeated the story laughed in his face.

He went outside the camp and brought back the head. Then indeed his parents rejoiced, for they knew that he would be admitted at once to the company of warriors for

having rid them of so great an enemy. While they all wondered how one who was so lazy could have become so great a brave, he told them why he had acted as he did before he left the village. He was so strong that he had been afraid of breaking things, and so did not dare to touch them. He took hold of some fishing nets, and as he turned them over in his fingers, they snapped in many places. But now that he was a man his strength would be useful to him and to the tribe. He could clear the forest of fallen trees, and carry some to the streams, where he could throw them so that his people might go from one side to the other in safety. Thereafter he was not known as White Hawk the Lazy, but as "The Strong Man."

The Magic
Feather

In the depths of the forest in the land of the Dacotahs stood a wigwam many leagues distant from any other. The old man who had been known to live in it was supposed to have died, but he kept himself in hiding for the sake of his little grandson, whose mother had brought him there to escape the giants.

The Dacotahs had once been a brave and mighty people. They were swift runners and proud of their fleetness. It had been told among the nations for many generations that a great chief should spring from this tribe, and that he should conquer all his enemies, even the giants who had made themselves strong by eating the flesh and drinking the blood of those they took in battle. This great chief should wear a white feather and should be known by its name.

The giants believed the story and sought to prevent it coming true. So they said to the Dacotahs: "Let us run a race. If you win you shall have our sons and our daughters to do with them as you please, and if we win we will take yours."

Some of the wise Indians shook their heads and said: "Suppose the giants win, they will kill our children and will serve them as food upon their tables." But the young men answered: "Kaw. Who can outrun the Dacotahs? We shall return from the race with the young giants bound hand and foot, to fetch and carry for us all our days." So they agreed to the wager and ran with the giants.

Now, it was not to be supposed that the giants would act fairly. They dug pitfalls on the prairie, covering them with leaves and grass, which caused the runners to stumble and lose the race.

The Dacotahs, therefore, had to bring out their children and give them to the giants. When they were counted, one child was missing. The giants roared with anger and made the whole tribe search for him, but he could not be found. Then the giants killed the father instead and ate his flesh, grumbling and muttering vengeance with every mouthful.

This was the child whose home was in the forest. When he was still a very little fellow his grandfather made him a tiny bow and some smooth, light arrows, and taught him how to use them.

The first time he ventured from the lodge he brought

home a rabbit, the second time a squirrel, and he shot a fine, large deer long before he was strong enough to drag it home.

One day when he was about fourteen years old, he heard a voice calling to him as he went through the thick woods: "Come hither, you wearer of the white feather. You do not yet wear it, but you are worthy of it."

He looked about, but at first saw no one. At last he caught sight of the head of a little old man among the trees. On going up to it he discovered that the body from the heart downward was wood and fast in the earth. He thought some hunter must have leaped upon a rotten stump and, it giving way, had caught and held him fast; but he soon recognized the roots of an old oak that he well knew. Its top had been blighted by a stroke of lightning, and the lower branches were so dark that no birds built their nests on them, and few even lighted upon them.

The boy knew nothing of the world except what his grandfather had taught him. He had once found some lodge poles on the edge of the forest and a heap of ashes like those about their own wigwam, by which he guessed that there were other people living. He had never been told why he was living with an old man so far away from others, or of his father, but the time had come for him to know these things.

The head, which had called him, said as he came near: "Go home, White Feather, and lie down to sleep. You will

dream, and on waking will find a pipe, a pouch of smoking mixture, and a long white feather beside you. Put the feather on your head, and as you smoke you will see the cloud which rises from your pipe pass out of the doorway as a flock of pigeons." The voice then told him who he was, and also that the giants had never given up looking for him. He was to wait for them no longer, but to go boldly to their lodge and offer to race with them. "Here," said the voice, "is an enchanted vine which you are to throw over the head of every one who runs with you."

White Feather, as he was thereafter called, picked up the vine, went quickly home and did as he had been told. He heard the voice, awoke and found the pouch of tobacco, the pipe, and the white feather. Placing the feather on his head, he filled the pipe and sat down to smoke.

His grandfather, who was at work not far from the wigwam, was astonished to see flocks of pigeons flying over his head, and still more surprised to find that they came from his own doorway. When he went in and saw the boy wearing the white feather, he knew what it all meant and became very sad, for he loved the boy so much that he could not bear the thought of losing him.

The next morning White Feather went in search of the giants. He passed through the forest, out upon the prairie, and through other woods across another prairie, until at last he saw a tall lodge pole in the middle of the forest. He went boldly up to it, thinking to surprise the giants, but his coming was not unexpected, for the little spirits which carry the news had heard the voice speaking to him and had hastened to tell those whom it most concerned.

The giants were six brothers who lived in a lodge that was ill-kept and dirty. When they saw the boy coming they made fun of him among themselves, but when he entered the lodge they pretended that they were glad to see him and flattered him, telling him that his fame as a brave had already reached them.

White Feather knew well what they wanted. He proposed the race, and though this was just what they had intended doing, they laughed at his offer. At last they said that if he would have it so, he should try first with the smallest and weakest of their number.

They were to run toward the east until they came to a certain tree which had been stripped of its bark, and then back to the starting point, where a war club made of iron was driven into the ground. Whoever reached this first was to beat the other's brains out with it.

White Feather and the youngest giant ran nimbly on, and the giants, who were watching, were rejoiced to see their brother gain slowly but surely, and at last shoot ahead of White Feather. When his enemy was almost at the goal, the boy, who was only a few feet behind, threw the enchanted vine over the giant's head, which caused him to fall back helpless. No one suspected anything more than an accident, for the vine could not be seen except by him who carried it.

70

After White Feather had cut off the giant's head, the brothers thought to get the better of him, and begged him to leave the head with them, for they thought that by magic they might bring it back to life, but he claimed his right to take it home to his grandfather.

The next morning he returned to run with the second giant, whom he defeated in the same manner; the third morning the third, and so on until all but one were killed.

As he went toward the giant's lodge on the sixth morning he heard the voice of the old man of the oak tree who had first appeared to him. It came to warn him. It told him that the sixth giant was afraid to race with him, and would therefore try to deceive him and work enchantment on him. As he went through the wood he would meet a beautiful woman, the most beautiful in the world. To avoid danger he must wish himself an elk and he would be changed into that animal. Even then he must keep out of her way, for she meant to do him harm.

White Feather had not gone far from the tree when he met her. He had never seen a woman before, and this one was so beautiful that he wished himself an elk at once, for he was sure she would bewitch him. He could not tear himself away from the spot, however, but kept browsing near her, raising his eyes now and then to look at her.

She went to him, laid her hand upon his neck and stroked his sides. Looking from him she sighed, and as he turned his head toward her, she reproached him for changing himself from a tall and handsome man to such an ugly creature. "For," said she, "I heard of you in a distant land, and, though many sought me, I came hither to be your wife."

As White Feather looked at her he saw tears shining in her eyes, and almost before he knew it he wished himself a man again. In a moment he was restored to his natural shape, and the woman flung her arms about his neck and kissed him.

By and by she coaxed him to lie down on the ground and put his head on her lap. Now, this beautiful woman was really the giant in disguise, and as White Feather lay with his head on her knee, she stroked his hair and forehead and by her magic put him to sleep. Then she took an ax and broke his back. This done, she changed herself into the giant, turned White Feather into a dog, and bade him follow to the lodge.

The giant took the white feather and placed it on his own head, for he knew there was magic in it, and he wished to make the tribes honor him as the great warrior they had long expected.

II

In a little village but a woman's journey from the home of the giants lived a chief named Red Wing. He had two daughters, White Weasel and Crystal Stone, each noted for

her beauty and haughtiness. Crystal Stone was kind to every
one but her lovers, who came from far and near, and were
a constant source of jealousy to White Weasel, the elder.
The eldest of the giants was White Weasel's suitor, but she
was afraid of him, so both the sisters remained unmarried.

When the news of White Feather's race with the giants
came to the village, each of the maidens determined that
she would win the young brave for a husband. White
Weasel wanted someone who would be a great chief and
make all the tribes afraid of him. Crystal Stone loved him
beforehand, for she knew he must be good as well as brave,
else the white feather would not have been given to him.
Each kept the wish to herself and went into the woods to
fast, so that it might come true.

When they heard that White Feather was on his way
through the forest, White Weasel set her lodge in order and
dressed herself gaily, hoping to attract his attention. Her
sister made no such preparation, for she thought so brave
and wise a chief would have too good sense to take notice
of a woman's finery.

When the giant passed through the forest, White Weasel
went out and invited him into her lodge. He entered and
she did not guess that it was the giant of whom she had
been in such fear.

Crystal Stone invited the dog into her lodge—her sister
had shut him out—and was kind to it, as she had always
been to dumb creatures. Now, although the dog was en-

chanted and could not change his condition, he still had more than human sense and knew all the thoughts of his mistress. He grew to love her more and more every day and looked about for some way to show it.

One day when the giant was hunting on the prairie, the dog went out to hunt also, but he ran down to the bank of the river. He stepped cautiously into the water and drew out a large stone, which was turned into a beaver as soon as it touched the ground. He took it home to his mistress, who showed it to her sister and offered to share it with her. White Weasel refused it, but told her husband he had better follow the dog and discover where such fine beavers could be had.

The giant went, and hiding behind a tree, saw the dog draw out a stone, which turned into a beaver. After the animal had gone home he went down to the water and drew out a stone, which likewise turned into a beaver. He tied it to his belt and took home, throwing it down at the door of the lodge.

When he had been at home a little while, he told his wife to go and bring in his belt. She did so, but there was no beaver tied to it, only a large, smooth stone such as he had drawn out of the water.

The dog, knowing that he had been watched, would not go for more beavers, but the next day went through the woods until he came to a charred tree. He broke off a small branch, which turned into a bear as soon as he took hold of it to carry it home. The giant, who had been watching him, also broke off a branch, and he, too, secured a bear. When he took it home and told his wife to fetch it in, she found a black stick.

The White Weasel became very angry and scoffed at her husband, asking him if this was the way he had done the wonderful things that had made his fame. "Ugh!" she said, "you are a coward, though you are so big and great."

The next day, after the giant had gone out, she went to the village to tell her father, Red Wing, how badly her husband treated her in not bringing home food. She also told him that her sister, who had taken the dog into her wigwam, always had plenty to eat, and that Crystal Stone pitied the wife of the wearer of the white feather, who often had to go hungry.

Red Wing listened to her story and knew at once that there must be magic at work somewhere. He sent a company of young men and women to the lodge of Crystal Stone to see if White Weasel's story were true, and if so to bring his younger daughter and the dog to his wigwam.

Meanwhile the dog had asked his mistress to give him a bath such as the Indians take. They went down to the river, where he pointed out a spot on which she was to build him a lodge. She made it of grass and sticks, and after heating some large stones laid them on the floor, leaving only just enough room for the dog to crawl in and lie down. Then she poured water on the stones, which caused

75

a thick steam that almost choked him. He lay in it for a long time, after which, raising himself, he rushed out and jumped into a pool of water formed by the river. He came out a tall, handsome man, but without the power of speech.

The messengers from Red Wing were greatly astonished at finding a man instead of the dog that they had expected to see, but had no trouble in persuading him and Crystal Stone to go with them.

Red Wing was as much astonished as his messengers had been, and called all the wise men of the tribe to witness what should take place, and to give counsel concerning his daughters.

The whole tribe and many strangers soon assembled. The giant came also and brought with him the magic pipe that had been given to White Feather in his dream. He smoked it and passed it to the Indians to smoke, but nothing came of it. Then White Feather motioned to them that he wished to take it. He also asked for the white feather, which he placed on his head. At the first whiff from the pipe, clouds of blue and white pigeons rushed from the smoke.

The men sprang to their feet, astonished to see such magic. White Feather's speech returned, and in answer to the questions put to him, he told his story to the chief.

Red Wing and the council listened and smoked for a time in silence. Then the oldest and wisest brave ordered the giant to appear before White Feather, who should trans-

76

form him into a dog. White Feather accomplished this by knocking upon him the ashes from the magic pipe. It was next decreed that the boys of the tribe should take the war clubs of their fathers and, driving the animal into the forest, beat him to death.

White Feather wished to reward his friends, so he invited them to a buffalo hunt, to take place in four days' time, and he bade them to prepare many arrows. To make ready for them, he cut a buffalo robe into strips, which he sowed upon the prairie.

On the day appointed the warriors found that these shreds of skin had grown into a large herd of buffaloes. They killed as many as they pleased, for White Feather tipped each arrow with magic so that none missed their aim.

A grand feast followed in honor of White Feather's triumph over the giants and of his marriage with Crystal Stone.

The Star
Maiden

THE OJIBWAYS were a great nation whom the fairies loved.
Their land was the home of many spirits, and as long as
they lived on the shores of the great lakes, the woods in
that country were full of fairies. Some of them dwelt in
the moss at the roots or on the trunks of trees. Others hid
beneath the mushrooms and toadstools. Some changed
themselves into bright-winged butterflies or tinier insects
with shining wings. This they did that they might be near
the children they loved, and play with them where they
could see and be seen.

But there were also evil spirits in the land. These burrowed in the ground, gnawed at the roots of the loveliest
flowers and destroyed them. They breathed upon the corn
and blighted it. They listened whenever they heard men

talking, and carried the news to those with whom it would make most mischief.

It is because of these fairies that the Indian must be silent in the woods and must not whisper confidences in the camp unless he is sure the spirits are fast asleep under the white blanket of the snow.

The Ojibways looked well after the interests of the good spirits. They shielded the flowers and stepped carefully aside when mosses or flowers were in their path. They brushed no moss from the trees, and they never snared the sunbeams, for on them thousands of fairies came down from the sky. When the chase was over they sat in the doorways of their wigwams smoking, and as they watched the blue circles drift and fade into the darkness of the evening, they listened to the voices of the fairies and the insects' hum and the thousand tiny noises that night always brings.

One night as they were listening they saw a bright light shining in the top of the tallest tree. It was a star brighter than all the others, and it seemed very near the earth. When they went close to the tree they found that it was really caught in the topmost branches.

The wise men of the tribe were summoned and for three nights they sat about the council fire, but they came to no conclusion about the beautiful star. At last one of the young warriors went to them and told them that the truth had come to him in a dream.

While asleep the west wind had lifted the curtains of

his wigwam and the light of the star fell full upon him. Suddenly a beautiful maiden stood at his side. She smiled upon him, and as he gazed speechless she told him that her home was in the star and that in wandering over all the earth she had seen no land so fair as the land of the Ojibways. Its flowers, its sweet-voiced birds, its rivers, its beautiful lakes, its mountains clothed in green—these had charmed her, and she wished to be no more a wanderer. If they would welcome her she would make her home among them, and she asked them to choose a place in which she might dwell.

The council was greatly pleased, but they could not agree upon what was best to offer the Star Maiden, so they decided to ask her to choose for herself.

She searched first among the flowers of the prairie. There she found the fairies' ring, where the little spirits danced on moonlit nights. "Here," thought she, "I will rest." But as she swung herself backward and forward on the stem of a lovely blossom, she heard a terrible noise and fled in great fear. A vast herd of buffaloes came and took possession of the fairies' ring, where they rolled over one another, and bellowed so they could be heard far on the trail. No gentle star maiden could choose such a resting place.

She next sought the mountain rose. It was cool and pleasant, the moss was soft to her dainty feet, and she could talk to the spirits she loved, whose homes were in the stars.

But the mountain was steep, and huge rocks hid from her view the nation that she loved.

She was almost in despair, when one day as she looked down from the edge of the wild rose leaf she saw a white flower with a heart of gold shining on the waters of the lake below her. As she looked, a canoe, steered by the young warrior who had told her wishes to his people, shot past, and his strong, brown hand brushed the edge of the flower.

"That is the home for me," she cried, and half-skipping, half-flying down the side of the mountain, she quickly made her way to the flower and hid herself in its bosom. There she could watch the stars as well as when she looked upward from the cup of the mountain rose; there she could talk to the star spirits, for they bathed in the clear lake; and best of all, there she could watch the people whom she loved, for their canoes were always upon the water.

The Great
Head

LONE WOLF was an Indian who, with his wife and ten
sons, moved some distance from their tribe and built themselves a lodge in the forest. The man and his wife were both
old, and when sickness came they had no strength to fight
it, but died within a few moons of each other. The sons
were too young to live by themselves, and therefore went
to the wigwam of their uncle, Deep Lake, their mother's
brother. He gave them food and shelter until the elder
ones were able to hunt and so provide for their brothers.

One morning several of them started out, each going in
a different direction. The eldest went toward the north,
because he was better able to travel far and to fight the
fierce animals which lived in that region.

The night came, bright with many stars, but he did not
return.

The next morning the second brother set out in the same direction, thinking he might find the trail of the other. He did not return. Then the third brother went in search of those who had disappeared, and he, too, was seen no more.

Thus they all followed one another, until only the youngest, Little Elk, was left with his uncle. He was too small and feeble to hope to succeed where his brothers had failed, and Deep Lake forbade him going out alone, for fear the witch or giant who had destroyed his brothers should do him harm.

One day while Deep Lake and Little Elk were in the woods together they heard a deep groan which seemed to come from the ground. They searched and found a man covered with mold and lying under a great log.

"Quick," said Deep Lake to his nephew, "run to the lodge and get the bear's oil."

Little Elk hurried to the wigwam and returned with a jar of bear's oil, with which he rubbed the man until he became conscious and was able to speak. His words were very strange, considering that he had never seen either of them before.

"You," said he, looking at the boy, "are Little Elk. You had nine brothers who set out toward the barren place to hunt, and not one of them ever returned."

The old man began to suspect magic, and asked, tremblingly, "Who are you?"

"I," said the stranger, "am Rotten Foot, the brother of the Great Head."

Deep Lake knew well about the Great Head. It was an enormous head without any body. It had large eyes that rolled about fearfully, and long, coarse hair like that of the grizzly bear, and it streamed over the huge cleft rock that was his home. Seen or unseen, if it caught sight of any living thing it would shriek in a shrill voice, "I see thee, I see thee. Thou shalt die!"

Deep Lake had been a brave chief, and he thought perhaps he could conquer the Great Head, or that at least he could find out about his nephews, whom he felt sure the Great Head had destroyed. The plan which occurred to him was to be kind to the Great Head's brother, so that he might learn more about him.

He therefore invited Rotten Foot to his wigwam, gave him the most comfortable seat by the fire, rubbed his stiff limbs with bear's oil, and set food before him.

When he was warm and well fed, Deep Lake began to question him about the Great Head. "Could you bring him here?" he said at last.

"He would not come merely for the asking, but I might lure him hither," was the reply.

The next day Rotten Foot set out in search of his brother. He promised to use all his skill and magic, if necessary, to bring him to the lodge. "Have ready some blocks of the maple tree for the Great Head's food, in case he should return with me," said he, as he set out on his journey.

He pulled up a hickory tree and made arrows of its roots. He then crept cautiously along until he saw the cleft rock

in the distance. Fearing that he might be seen, he used his magic and crawled inside a mole and told the animal to burrow into the ground, so as to hide him.

It was not long before he heard the Great Head growl, "I see thee, I see thee. Thou shalt die!"

Rotten Foot looked out and saw that his brother was watching an owl, which immediately dropped from the tree, its flesh crumbled and its bones immediately lay bare.

Rotten Foot drew out an arrow and aimed it at his brother. It was but a small arrow when it started, but it grew larger and larger as it neared the Great Head. It did not strike him, but flew back, growing smaller and smaller until it was its original size, and slipped itself into the quiver at Rotten Foot's side.

Feeling sure that the Great Head would follow him, he turned and ran toward Deep Lake's wigwam. The ridge that the mole made as it passed along completely hid him from the view of the Great Head, who soon followed in a roaring tempest.

Deep Lake heard him tearing through the forest, and provided himself and Little Elk with war clubs in case he should attack the wigwam.

Just as Rotten Foot reached the wigwam and was about to jump out of the mole's skin, the Great Head recognized his brother. He was delighted to see him, for he had long since supposed him dead. He laughed so loudly that the clouds were broken and a rainbow appeared above the trees.

On hearing the change in his voice, from fierce anger to laughter, Deep Lake and Little Elk dropped their clubs and brought out the blocks of the maple tree.

The Great Head devoured them greedily, and when he had finished he told them that he had made up his mind to kill a witch who lived toward the north, and who destroyed twice as many animals and men as he did. "I never kill the brave or the innocent," said he, "but she has no mercy, and draws men to their death by her sweet songs. They lull the unwary hunter as the snow lulls him when he staggers and falls in the forest."

Deep Lake then said, "Let me go with you, for the witch has slain my nephews, nine men, all brothers of this lad."

"No," said the Great Head. "I will take the boy, and he shall help to avenge their death."

They traveled in the night, and early in the morning came in sight of the witch's lodge. It was a cave filled with dead men's bones. Their fingers hung from the roof, their scalps were heaped together for her couch, their skulls were her bowls and kettles.

She sat rocking herself to and fro, singing a low, sweet song, the notes of which made all who heard it turn cold and shiver till all their flesh was shaken off them and they became nothing but dry bones.

The Great Head had told Little Elk to put two clover blossoms into his ears so that he could not hear her. When they were near her lodge he said to the lad: "I will ask her the question, 'How long have you been here?' This will break the charm of her song upon me, but you will see the hair fall from my head. You must put it back as fast as it comes out and it will grow at once and very long. Then I will jump upon her and bite her. You must take the pieces of flesh from my mouth and throw them from you, saying, 'Be a fox, a bird,' or anything you choose, so they will run off and never return."

As they crept up to the cave, the Great Head shouted, "How long have you been here?"

His hair began to fall out in long, thick locks, which Little Elk at once replaced. The Great Head then jumped upon the witch, and she screamed and begged for mercy; but he answered, "You had no mercy on others; you must die!"

He bit her and killed her, and all the plain was covered with animals and the river was filled with fish from the pieces of her body. To make sure of her never coming to life again, they burned her bones and scattered them on the river.

Then the Great Head told Little Elk to search for the year-old bones, which would be whiter than the others, and lay them together. "Now," said he, "I am going home, and as I go I will raise a tempest that will strike into the mouth of this cave. As it touches the bones, you must say, 'All arise.'"

Little Elk had just laid down the last bone when he

89

heard the wind rising in the forest. As it blew into the cave he called loudly, "All arise!"

The bones stood up and were immediately covered with flesh. The brothers recognized one another, and one and all praised Little Elk for his courage and his patience. Then they vanished down the trail into the forest.

The Fighting
Hare

THE PRINCE of the Hares was playing with his children in front of his burrow one day, when, growing tired, he threw back his ears, drew in his feet, and lay down to sleep.

Meanwhile the sun came up and passed so close to the earth that it burnt his back full of holes. The Hare felt very sore, and as he rubbed himself, his fur came off in great patches so that his beauty was spoiled. He was furiously angry, and starting up, cried out that he would fight the sun. In spite of all that his friends could say, the Hare went at once in pursuit of him.

The land where the Hare lived was a vast plain. When he had come to the end of it, he climbed a high hill in order to look over the country. He saw below him on the other side a field of green plumes nodding to the west wind. He had never seen corn growing before, and did not know what these plumes were.

He ran eagerly to the place, broke off as many as he could carry, and hid them behind the rocks. Then he rubbed two dead branches together and made a fire, in which he roasted the corn.

Presently the owner came along, and seeing the damage done, called his warriors to fight the thief.

The Hare had burrowed a hole at the side of the rock, and when the arrows were hurled at him, he blew them back with his magic breath. The warriors ran to catch him, but so great was their haste that one rushed upon another, and each caught only the other's fists. Then they thought of digging him out. They worked until the Sun Prince was half way home, but before they had caught sight of the Hare, he had escaped through a secret passage.

He ran to a rock a little way off and higher than the one beneath which they were digging, and hurled his magic ball at the burrow, breaking away the floor and the sides, so that it fell in, burying the Chief and all his followers.

The next morning the Hare saw two men making arrow-heads of hot rocks. He watched them heating the rocks, and when they were red hot, he cried out: "O ho! Hot rocks will not burn me!"

The men looked up, and one of them said: "Are you a wizard?"

"No," said the Hare, "but I am a better man than you are, or the man who is working with you. I will lie on the hot rocks, if you will let me hold you on them in the same manner."

They agreed. So, when the rocks were glowing, the Hare laid himself on top of them, and the men pressed him down against them with their hands. But he breathed heavily, and his magic breath so cooled the part on which he was lying that not a particle of his fur was singed.

The men, having no such protection, soon begged for mercy, but the Hare held them to their promise and they both perished. "So much for making one's self equal to a wizard," said the Hare to himself as he continued his journey.

The following day he passed by a high cliff round which the winds blew so hard that it was known by the men of that country as Hurricane Cliff. It overhung a deep ravine in which were sunflowers as tall as trees and the heads were heavy with seeds.

The Hare took a handful of seeds and amused himself by throwing them into the air and catching them in his mouth. While doing this he heard voices, and looking up, saw a group of women who were plotting to kill him.

"O ho!" they said, "let us call the hurricane to hurl a rock down on him."

The Hare said nothing, but went in full sight of them and began eating the seeds with great relish. The women looked at them longingly, and finally asked him to share his food with them, not knowing what he really had.

He tossed a handful of seeds into the air, and they tried

hard to catch them, but failed again and again, each time going nearer to the edge of the cliff till, in her eagerness, the one nearest the edge reached out too far and fell into the ravine. The others were so close that they fell over her; so all but two were dashed to pieces, and these vowed vengeance on the Hare.

He met them soon afterward gathering berries, and called out that he would give them the revenge they wished. "Come," said he, "you may blow those blackberry thorns and leaves into my eyes. I will let you try first and if you do not blind me you must let me do the same to you."

They took him at his word and threw a handful of little else than thorns. But by breathing as he had done when on the hot rocks, he blew them all from him.

The women trusted their hands to protect them, but the Hare aimed well and the thorns passed between their fingers and put their eyes out.

He had one more adventure with women. While passing through a lonely place he saw several women weaving jugs of willow which they made watertight by smearing them inside with pitch. They, too, were planning to destroy him.

He went boldly up to them and proposed that they should put him inside one of the jugs. As he could not get into those already made they put him into one that was not finished and wove the neck of the jug about him, making it very small, so that he should not escape.

While they were laughing at the ease with which he had been caught, he burst the jug open and stepped out unhurt.

He then compelled them to get inside of the jugs and to let him weave the necks about them. He worked slowly at first to make them think that he did not know how to weave, but he made the necks strong and fastened them well.

Then he rolled the jugs about till the women were shaken and badly bruised. They threatened to be revenged, but when he knocked them harder and their blood ran out over the ground, they begged him to let them out.

He would not, but, after a time, thinking that they had suffered enough, he struck each jug with his magic ball and put them out of their misery.

A tarantula who had watched the Hare resolved to punish him by his own methods. The spider had a magic club which poisoned everything it struck, but never injured him. He called to the Hare and asked to be struck with the club.

The Hare raised it and beat him on the head and back, but the spider remained unhurt. He began to suspect something wrong, and just before it was his turn to be struck he changed the spider's club for his magic ball and killed the insect with one blow.

Thus he traveled on, conquering all who opposed him or plotted against him, till he came to the edge of the world. There he saw a high cliff covered with trees of all sizes and kinds. He went up to the maple and said: "What are you good for, pray?"

The maple shook its leaves in great disdain and said: "I

am the food of the Great Head. The blood of my children is sweet and nourishing, and they give it freely to the nations."

The Hare next went to the larch and asked: "What are you good for?"

"I," said the larch, "bind together the canoes of the people. If it were not for me they could not sail upon the lakes and rivers."

The cedar answered the question by saying: "I make the canoes strong, so that they will bear the weight of the great warriors. If it were not for me, none but women and children could sail on the waters."

The birch stood next in his way and said: "If it were not for me you could make no canoes at all. My bark is for the picture-writing of the people. How, but for me, could one Chief talk to his brother who lives by the distant river?"

The fir tree boasted of its balsam without which the canoe could not glide upon the water.

"Ugh!" said the Hare. "You all say that no canoe could be made without you. You, linden, you have no part in these canoes. What are you good for?"

"I," said the linden, "am for the cradles of the children. Without me where could they be rocked and put to sleep when the beautiful red has gone from the sky and the night comes? From me you take the basswood for your bowls and your drinking cups."

The oak stood in his path, and before the question was

96

put to it, touched his head with its lower branches and said in a deep voice: "I shelter the great warriors. I mark the spot for their councils. From my boughs are made the swift arrows that bring food to the feet of the hunter and carry death to his enemies."

The ash sighed and whispered: "From me is taken the bow that speeds the arrow in its flight."

The red willow drooped its head as it said: "My bark is for the pipe of the Indian, my wands are to bid him to the feast. My osiers are for his baskets, his mats, and his water jugs."

Thus every tree claimed to be of so much use that men could not do without it. At last the Hare came to a little tree hardly more than a shrub, many of whose leaves were blighted. "Of what use are you?" asked he.

"None," said the tree, "unless you can use me."

"We shall see, we shall see," said the Hare.

He went to the top of the cliff and saw the sun just rising. It caught sight of him at the same moment, and knowing that he had come for vengeance, it retreated quickly into its cave.

It stayed there three days and all the world suffered from cold and darkness. At last the noise of the people in their discontent reached the sun and he was obliged to come out.

The Hare had his arrows ready and aimed many at him, but they fell short of their mark. When the sun was directly overhead he drew forth a magic arrow, which he dipped

into a magic tear that escaped from his eye. With this he took good aim. It struck the sun and broke it into thousands of fragments.

The flying pieces set the whole world on fire. It burned the forest, the prairie, the villages, the corn and the wild rice, the pumpkin vines and the gourds, the grapes and the nuts.

The children of the Hare Prince ran into their burrow and the Great Elk led many of the other animals into a vast field in the Rocky Mountains, around which was drawn a sacred line that no fire could cross.

The fire burned the cliff at the edge of the world. The Hare sought refuge first in one tree and then in another, but they were all destroyed except the little one that had said it was of no use. It was so small that it could not wholly protect him. His tail, his back, his feet, and the tips of his ears were burned, every part of him except his head.

He rolled over and over trying to get relief, but his pain was so great that his eyes burst, and the water gushing from them put out the fire.

The sun had been conquered and was summoned to appear before the council. They found him guilty of cruelty and indifference to the welfare of men; so he was compelled to travel the same trail day after day for all time and at a fixed distance from the earth. Thus he can no longer burn trees or animals, nor can he leave them in cold and darkness.

The Adventures
of Living Statue

LIVING STATUE was a great magician of the Ottawas, who lived on the shores of Lake Huron. His wigwam was of skin that had been scrubbed and bleached until it shone like snow when the sun falls upon it, and it could be seen at a great distance. From the lodge pole downward it was covered with paintings, some done by the magician and others by his friends, each telling a wonderful tale of his magic.

His couch was of white buffalo skins, which are very rare and precious. His pipes were the admiration of all who saw them, for they were ornamented with red feathers from the breast of the robin, blue from the jay, purple from the neck of the pigeon, and green from the throat of the drake. His moccasins of rabbit skin, dyed scarlet, were the softest that could be made. They were worked with beads brought by

100

a messenger from a far-distant tribe, who had received them from the Palefaces that came across the Big Salt Lake. But the most wonderful thing about these moccasins was that they were magic shoes; for every stride he took in them carried him over a mile of ground.

His flute was a reed cut in the swamp forest. When he blew a loud note upon it the distant rocks answered him, and the little vanishing men who danced in the moonlight took up the music and laughed it back to him. When he breathed softly upon it no Indian heard him, for the sound went straight into the heart of the flowers. The fairies hearing it crept forth and balanced themselves on the petals of the flowers that they might hear the better.

The magician's sister, Sweet Strawberry, whose fawn-skin robe may be seen in the moon on bright nights, sometimes rested on the topmost branches of the tall trees to listen. She had once lived with him, but the Moon Prince had taken her to be his bride, and all the tribe mourned for her as for one dead.

Living Statue talked with the birds and the squirrels, who laid down and died and rolled out of their skins when he asked for them. He was the friend of all the rabbits, who were proud to have him eat them. When he had finished the meal, he read the story of the animal's life in its bones, and if it had been good in its time he stroked its skin and it came to life again, and could nevermore be caught.

One day, as Living Statue was walking across the plain

near the edge of the forest, he met a little man no higher than his knee. The dwarf was dressed all in green, and wore a green cap with a red plume in it.

"Fight me, fight me," said the dwarf, placing himself directly in front of the magician.

Living Statue tried to kick him out of his path. Thereupon his foot began to swell so that he could hardly move.

"Fight me, fight me," said the dwarf, who again danced in front of him.

Living Statue stooped and took hold of him, intending to throw him to one side, but he found the dwarf too strong for him. He strove in vain to lift him, so he wrestled with him till his arms were tired, but the dwarf was not overcome. At last, by a great effort he pushed him from him, then rushed at him with all his might and succeeded in throwing him to the ground. He sprang quickly upon him, and taking out his knife prepared to scalp him.

"Hold, hold," said the dwarf, "I see the Ottawa magician is a brave warrior, as well as a great wizard. He has fought and conquered me, though not by magic. I will show him greater magic than any he has ever known."

When he had done speaking he threw himself backward and was changed into a crooked ear of corn, which rolled over and lay at the magician's feet.

"Take me," said the ear. "Tear off the wrapper that is drawn so tightly about me and leave nothing to hide my body from your eyes. Then pull my body to pieces, taking

all the flesh from the bones and throw the flesh upon different parts of the plain. Cover me with earth that the ravens may not feast upon me. My spine you shall break in pieces no longer than your thumb and shall scatter them near the edge of the forest. Go back to your village when you have done this and return to this place after one moon."

Living Stone did exactly what the dwarf had told him to do, but he said nothing to the Ottawas about his adventure. It was not for them to understand magic. They might try to do what he alone understood and the spirits would be offended.

When the Hot Moon had come Living Statue went back to the plain where he had wrestled with the dwarf, and he saw a field of long, green plumes waving in the sunlight. They were smooth and glossy and dropped almost to the ground. In color they were like the robe of the dwarf, only bright and shining.

While he was looking and wondering, the dwarf suddenly sprang out of the broadest stalk and said, "You have done well. Let one moon pass and another appear before you come again. Then you will find a new food for the Ottawas, better than the wild rice, sweet as the blood of the maple, and strength-giving as the flesh of the deer."

At the time appointed, Living Statue went again to the spot and there he found the gift of the corn. He brought his tribe to witness, and to gather it. Then he and three other magicians painted their bodies with white clay and danced round the kettle in which it was being prepared. When done, they took out the ears and burned them as a sacrifice. They then put out the fire and lighted a fresh one, with which they cooked "the spirits' berry" for themselves.

One night when Living Statue lay asleep, he heard the curtain of his tent flap, and presently two dwarfs entered and crept up to his couch. One climbed upon his legs and sat astride them. The other mounted to his breast and began feeling his throat.

"Choke him! Choke him!" said the dwarf at his feet.

"I can't. My hands are too small and weak," said the other.

"Pull his heart out! Pull his heart out!" said the first.

The second dwarf began pounding and tugging at the breast of the sleeper. At this the one astride his legs gave his companion a vicious kick, and said in a hoarse whisper, "You stupid! Pull it out through his mouth."

So the dwarf forced open the teeth of Living Statue and thrust his fingers far down his throat. Now, this was just what the magician thought he would do; so when the fingers were inside his mouth, he shut his teeth together quickly and bit them off. Then, slowly raising himself, he threw the dwarf who was on his legs clear to the door of the wigwam.

"Oh! oh!" cried the one whose hand was bitten, and he howled like a dog. "Oh! oh!" cried the other, and he howled like a wolf as the two disappeared in the darkness.

105

The magician kept very still, then crept to the door, raised the curtain, and put his head outside to listen, so that he might know in what direction they went. He heard them hurrying through the forest toward the lake. There was a soft splash, as of water when a canoe bends to it beneath the weight of a man, and all was still.

In the morning Living Statue found that the fingers he had bitten off were long wampum beads, greatly prized by the Indians, and so valuable that they made him very rich. He had no trouble in following the trail of the dwarfs, for it was marked by drops of blood that were changed into wampum beads. He had enough to make a coat, a cap and leggings, so that ever after he was known to all nations as the Prince of Wampum.

When he reached the lake he saw a stone canoe which was four times the length of his prow and white as the waves when the strong wind races with them to the shore. Two men were seated in it, one at the bow and the other in the stern. They were bolt upright, with their hands upon their knees, and did not look toward him. On going closer he saw that they were the dwarfs turned into stone. The boat was filled with sacks of bearskin, in which was treasure such as the magician had never before seen or imagined.

As he was about to take some of it away, the dwarf whose fingers he had bitten off, spoke to him and said: "In this manner the canoes of your people shall be loaded as they go past these shores, and no enemy shall be able to rob them."

The magician took the statues to his wigwam and afterward they were set up in the sacred lodge of the tribe, the white canoe being placed between them.

Many chiefs wished to give the Prince of Wampum their daughters in marriage, but he chose a star maiden, and they went to live in the fields of the sky, near the white, misty road of the dead.

Turtle Dove, Sage Cock, and the Witch

TURTLE DOVE was a widow with two children—Yellow Bird, a girl eleven years of age, and Sage Cock, a baby boy. The girl was big, awkward and stupid, but the boy, though only a baby, gave signs of being a remarkably bright child.

Turtle Dove was always anxious about him, for an old witch who lived in that part of the country stole every little boy that she could find.

One day Turtle Dove went down to the valley to gather seeds and herbs. She carried her baby on her back, but he was heavy, and after a time she grew tired from the weight and constant stooping. So she took the baby and laid him under a sagebrush, telling his sister to watch him.

Presently the old witch came that way, and going up to

the bundle, felt it all over, and asked Yellow Bird what it contained.

"It is my sister," said she, for she thought the witch would not want to steal a girl.

Then the old witch scolded her, growing more and more loud and angry in her speech and manner until her eyes stood out, glaring at the girl, and her grizzled locks rattled like the naked branches of the trees. Yellow Bird grew cold as ice and could not even scream she was so frightened.

The old witch, seeing that she was not likely to be attacked, seized the little papoose and flew away with him on her bat-like wings to the distant mountain, which no man can climb because of the rattlesnake forest at its base.

When she reached her den, which was a hollow place black with cinders and hidden from sight by a clump of hemlock trees, she laid the boy on the ground, broke the strips of deer skin that held his fur blanket over him, and stretched his legs till he became a man.

"Now," said she, "I shall have a husband."

Although Sage Cock had suddenly grown to a man's size, he had only a baby's heart and knew no better than to marry an ugly old witch.

When Turtle Dove returned and heard Yellow Bird's story she was very angry and would not forgive the girl for not calling her. She spent day after day searching among the rocks and wherever a wild beast or a witch might have a hiding place. She left no clump of bushes, however small,

unexplored, but all to no purpose. At last she went to her brother, Eagle, and told him her story.

Eagle was keen of sight and a swift hunter. He put on his war feathers and his war paint and set out in search of the boy.

One day he heard a baby crying, but he did not recognize its voice. He told his sister, and she begged him to take her to the place, for she felt sure that she would know the child's voice and he would know hers.

They went toward the witch's mountain. Before they reached it they heard the child cry, but did not know how to get to him because of the rattlesnake forest.

Eagle thought he would try his magic, for he was one of the wizards of the tribe. He took two feathers from his headdress and spread them out into wings, which he fastened upon his shoulders. He then placed Turtle Dove on his back and flew with her over the forest of rattlesnakes.

He hid in some bushes while the mother called, "Sage Cock, Sage Cock."

The child cried and tried to get out of the den. He did struggle through the bushes, but the witch caught him. Then with one blow of her stick she killed a mountain sheep nearby, and taking the boy in her arms, jumped into its stomach. She pulled the wool about them and lay very still.

Meanwhile Eagle killed a rabbit and put it on the top of a tall pine tree, then peeled the bark so that it would be hard to climb. They watched for days but with no success.

At last the old woman grew hungry, and Sage Cock cried for food. So she crept out, and seeing the rabbit, tried to get it.

When Eagle saw her he knew the baby could not be far off. He stretched himself full length on the ground and listened, with his ear to the earth.

First he heard a faint cry which seemed to come from the sheep, then, as he went nearer, he heard the boy's heart thumping and knew just where to go. He found the baby, caught him up in his arms, and ran quickly with him down to the edge of the rattlesnake forest.

Knowing the old witch would follow him, he raised a great snowstorm that covered all his tracks, so that she should not know in what direction he had gone.

But in his haste he dropped two eagle's feathers, and the witch knew at once who had stolen her husband. She went to her brother, one of the chiefs of the rattlesnakes, and asked him to take her part. He hated her, for she was always getting him into trouble, but she was his sister, and he could not refuse.

Just then, Eagle's war whoop was heard. The chief of the rattlesnakes, having no place in which to hide the witch, opened his mouth, and let her jump down his throat. She would not be still and bothered him so much that after Eagle had passed he tried to throw her off. But he could not rid himself of her, and at last he wrenched himself so hard that he jumped out of his own skin.

The witch still lives in it and rolls about among the rocks to this day, mocking all who pass, though no one can ever lay hold of her. The Palefaces call her Echo.

Sage Cock became a little boy again and grew to be a mighty chief, succeeding his uncle, Eagle, as a warrior and magician.

The Island
of Skeletons

BIG WAVE and his little nephew, Red Shell, lived together
in a deep forest. The boy was the only relative that the old
man had, and he was very fond of him. He had brought
Red Shell and his sister, Wild Sage, to his home some years
before, just after the great plague had killed most of his
tribe, among them the father and mother of the children.
But they had not been many months in the forest before
Wild Sage was stolen by a giant who lived on the Island of
Skeletons.

Big Wave warned the boy never to go toward the east;
for, if by any chance, he should cross a certain magic line
of sacred meal that Big Wave had drawn, he would be at
the mercy of the giant.

The boy obeyed for a time. By-and-by he grew tired of

playing in one place, so he went toward the east, not noticing when he crossed the magic line, till he came to the shore of a great lake.

He amused himself for a while, throwing pebbles into the water, and shooting arrows. A man came up to him, and said, "Well, boy, where is your lodge?"

Red Shell told him. Then the man proposed shooting arrows to see who could shoot the higher. Red Shell had had much practice, and though he was only a boy, his arm was strong, and he drew the bow far back and sent the arrow much higher than the man did.

The man laughed and said, "You are a brave boy. Now let us see whether you can swim as well as you can shoot."

They jumped into the water and tried holding their breath while swimming. Again the boy proved himself the victor.

When they were again on land, the man said to him, "Will you go with me in my canoe? I am on my way to an island where there are pretty birds, and you can shoot as many as you please."

Red Shell said he would go, and looked about for a canoe. The man began singing, and presently there appeared a canoe drawn by six white swans, three on either side. The boy and his companion stepped in and the man guided the swans by singing.

The island was so long that he could not see the end of it, but it was not very wide. It was thickly wooded and there was so much undergrowth that the ground could hardly be seen, but Red Shell noticed heaps of bones under the bushes, and asked what they were. He was told that the island had once been a famous hunting ground and these were the bones of the animals that had been killed.

After wandering about for some time, the man proposed another swim. They had been in the water but a few minutes when the boy heard singing, and looking around he saw the man going off in the canoe and taking his own and Red Shell's clothes with him. He shouted, but neither the man nor the birds paid any attention to him.

Thus he was left alone and naked, and it was fast growing dark. Then he remembered his uncle's warnings, and was so miserable from cold, hunger, and fear, that at last he sat down and cried.

By-and-by he heard a voice calling to him, "Hist! Keep still."

He looked around and saw a skeleton lying on the ground not far from him. It beckoned to him and said, "Poor boy, it was the same with me, but I will help you if you will do me a service. Go to that tree" (pointing to one close by), "dig on the west side of it, and you will find a pouch of smoking mixture and a pipe. Bring them to me. You can get a flint on the shore. Bring that also."

The boy was terribly frightened, but the skeleton spoke kindly, and not as though he meant to do harm. Red Shell therefore went to the tree, and brought the pipe and smok-

116

ing mixture. Then he found a flint and, on being asked to do so, struck fire, lit the pipe, and handed it to the skeleton.

It smoked quickly, drawing the smoke into the mouth and letting it escape between the ribs. Red Shell watched and saw mice run out from between the bones. When the skeleton was rid of them it said: "Now I feel better, and can tell you what to do to escape my fate. A giant is coming tonight with three dogs, to hunt you and kill you for his supper. You must lose the trail for them by jumping into the water many times on your way to a hollow tree, which you will find on the other side of the island. In the morning after they have gone, come to me."

Red Shell thanked the skeleton and started at once to find the tree. It was quite dark, so he could see nothing, but he ran from tree to tree, climbing halfway up each one, and running into the water many times before he found the place where he had been told to sleep.

Toward morning he heard the splash of a canoe in the water, and soon a giant, followed by three large dogs, strode into the forest.

"You must hunt this animal," the giant said to the dogs.

They scented the trail and dashed through the bushes. They rushed up one tree and then another, and at last came back to the giant with their tails between their legs, for they had found nothing.

He was so angry that he struck the foremost animal with his war club and killed it on the spot. He skinned it

117

and ate it raw. Then he drove the two others down to the canoe, jumped in, and went away.

When they were out of sight of the island, Red Shell crept from his hiding place and went back to the skeleton.

"You are still alive?" it asked in surprise. "You are a brave boy. Tonight the man who brought you here will come to drink your blood. You must go down to the shore before the darkness comes and dig a pit in the sand. Lie down in it and cover yourself with sand. When he leaves his canoe, get into it and say 'Come swans, let us go home.' If the man calls you, you must not turn around or look at him. When you are free, do not forget the skeleton."

Red Shell promised to come back to the island and to do all that he could for the poor bones. He went down to the shore and dug the pit deep enough so that when he stood in it his head was on a level with the water. When he heard the song in the distance he knew the swans were coming; so he covered his head with sand and waited till he heard a footstep on the dry leaves.

Then he crept out stealthily, stepped into the canoe, and whispered to the swans, "Come, let us go home." He began the song that he had heard their master sing to them, and the canoe glided from the shore.

The swans carried him down the lake to a large cleft rock in the center. They drew the canoe through the opening and through the cave till they came to a stone door. Red Shell tried to open it, but could not. Then he turned the canoe around and struck the door with the stern.

The door flew open and Red Shell found himself in a fine lodge. He saw his own clothes and many others heaped in a corner near the fire which was burning brightly. A kettle of soup was steaming over it and there were some potatoes in the ashes on the hearth.

Seeing no one, the boy ate supper and then lay down to sleep on a couch of wildcat skins.

In the morning he went out and stepping into the canoe, said, "Come swans, let us go to the island."

He saw the two dogs lying asleep in the sun and, on landing, found that they had killed their master.

The skeleton was delighted to see him and praised him for his courage and for being true to his word. But he said to him, "You must not go home yet. Travel toward the east three days and you will come to some huge rocks. There you will see a young girl drawing water from a spring. She is your sister, Wild Sage, whom the giant stole many moons since, and whom you believed dead. You will be able to get her away. When you have done so, come back to me."

Red Shell at once set out for the east and in three days he found the rocks of which he had been told. As he came near them he saw a lovely girl drawing water. "Sister," he said, going up to her, "you must come home with me."

She was frightened and tried to run away. Looking back, she saw that it was really her brother, and was even more afraid, though she turned and spoke to him. "Hist," said she, "a giant keeps me here. Go before he sees you or he will kill you."

Red Shell did not move.

"Go," said Wild Sage.

"No," he answered, "not till you go with me. Take me to your lodge."

The giant had gone to a cranberry swamp and Wild Sage knew that he would not return until the evening; so she ventured to take her brother home with her. She dug a pit in one corner of the lodge, told him to get into it, and then covered it with her bed of buffalo skins.

Just before the darkness came the giant's dogs rushed in, barking furiously.

"Who" said the giant, "is hidden here?"

"No one," said Wild Sage.

"There is, there is," said the giant, "or the dogs would not bark like that."

They did not discover Red Shell, however, so the giant sat down to his supper.

"This boy is not tender, he is not cooked enough, get up and cook him more," said the giant.

"Cook it yourself, if it doesn't suit you," she answered.

The giant took no notice of her answer, but called to her to come and take off his moccasins.

"Take them off yourself," she said.

"Kaw," thought the giant, "now I know she has someone hidden. I will kill him in the morning."

Early the next day the giant said he was going to the cranberry swamp to get some children for his dinner. He did not go far from the lodge, but hid himself in some bushes close to the shore.

He saw Wild Sage and her brother get into a canoe, and threw a hook after them, which caught the boat and drew it toward the shore. But Red Shell took up a stone and broke the hook, and they floated off once more.

The giant was in a terrible rage. He lay down flat on the ground, and, putting his mouth to the water, drank so fast that the canoe was drawn close to the shore. He began to swell from drinking such a quantity, and could not move. Red Shell took another stone and threw it at him. It struck him and snapped in two, and the water he swallowed flowed back into the lake.

Red Shell and his sister then sailed to the island, where the two dogs who had eaten their master rushed down to meet them. The boy raised his hand threateningly, and said: "Off to the woods as wolves. You no longer deserve to be dogs."

The animals slunk away growling, and as they disappeared were seen to change into lean and hungry wolves.

Red Shell went to the skeleton, who commanded him to gather all the bones that he could find on the island and to lay them side by side in one place. Then he was to say to them, "Dead folk, arise!"

It took him and his sister many days, for there were

122

bones everywhere. When all had been arranged in one place, Red Shell stood off at a distance and called loudly, "Dead folk, arise!" The bones raised themselves and took human form. All the men had bows and arrows, but some had only one arm, and others only one leg. The skeleton whom Red Shell had first met became a tall, handsome warrior, perfect in every limb. He saluted Red Shell as Chief, and the others did the same.

Then the boy and his sister crossed the lake and traveled westward till they came to their uncle's lodge. He was very old, his fire was out, and he was still mourning for his nephew. But as he listened to the story of the lad's adventures, and realized that he had come back unhurt, some of his years left him.

They built a long lodge with many fireplaces. Red Shell then returned to the island and brought back those who had been skeletons. The handsome brave, who was known as White Eagle, married Wild Sage, and they all dwelt together in peace to the end of their lives.

Stone Shirt
and the One-Two

STONE SHIRT was a terrible giant who wore a shirt of shells so fastened that no arrow could pierce it. He lived with his three daughters on the shore of the Big Sea Water.

His daughters were not bad or hardhearted, but they were forced to do all sorts of evil to protect their father. They had magic arrows which went wherever they wished and found their way straight to the hearts of their enemies, though shot without aim.

Stone Shirt, while out hunting one day, saw a beautiful woman gathering flags. "Who are you?" he said to her.

She was afraid of him, and said, "I am Spearmint."

"You are not," roared the giant, "you are Mouse, the wife of the Crane. I will kill him and you shall live with me. Kill your child before I return or I will dash him to pieces before your eyes."

Mouse picked up the boy, and as soon as the giant was out of sight she ran quickly with him to his grandmother's. Then she went back and smeared the stones with the blood of some fresh bear's meat which she threw into the lake.

She could not warn her husband, for he had gone hunting soon after sunrise, and she did not know which way he went or when he would be likely to return. Search as she might there was no escape.

The giant was not long gone, and when he returned he carried the scalp of the Crane, whom he had met on the way back to his wigwam. Seizing Mouse by the hair, he shook the scalp in her face, and then dragged her through the forest.

The deer had shed his horns many times when the baby boy, now grown to be a fine lad, went with his grandmother to dig flag roots. They took a sharp flint knife with which to cut the ground, for the roots are hard to pull.

When they had been some time in the swamp, they found that the roots came up easily and then more easily till at last they had only to take hold of a flag to have it at once loosened from the earth. The old woman said, "Surely something strange is going to happen. Let us go home, I do not care to dig any more today."

The boy took an armful of flags to the place where he had put the others, but the pile was gone. He called to his

grandmother and asked her if she had moved the roots.

"No, my child," said she, "perhaps some giant has stolen them. Let us go home."

The boy looked around and soon spied a man sitting under a tree not far off. He felt sure it was he who had stolen the flags, and taking up some small stones, threw them at him, calling him, "Thief! Coward!"

The man did not move. At last a stone larger than the others struck his leg and broke it. He lifted up the leg, bound it tightly with a strip torn from his coat, and again sat down under the tree. Then he beckoned to the boy, and pointing to some bones in front of him, asked: "What bones are these?"

The boy answered promptly, "Elk or deer."

"No," said the man, "these are the bones of your father. Has not the old woman told you how he was killed by Stone Shirt and his bones left to rot like those of the wolf?"

"No," said the boy.

"Has she not told you of your mother whom Stone Shirt carried off?"

"No," said the lad again. The man saw he would fight the giant, so he said no more, but disappeared as suddenly as he had come.

The boy went back to his grandmother and told her what he had heard. She knew at once that he must have seen a spirit. When the boy blamed her for keeping the story of his father's death a secret, she cried and said, "You

127

are my only hope. If you go to fight Stone Shirt, he will kill you and I shall be alone."

The boy made no answer, but went and lay down on his couch of skins, for he felt a heavy sleep coming over him. He slept three days and three nights. When he awoke he refused food and said, "I am going to all nations to enlist warriors in my cause," and passed out of the wigwam.

The boy was tall and well-formed, and while he slept he had taken on the face of a young man. He traveled many moons, and wherever he went the chiefs listened to him, and the young men of the different tribes took up their bows and arrows and declared themselves ready to follow him. Among them were two magicians, the Wolf and the Rattlesnake.

These two went with him some distance, and the three entered his grandmother's wigwam. After they had eaten a meal which the old woman gladly prepared for them, the young man took a stone axe and handing it to her asked her to cut him in two.

She refused, but he persisted, and at last commanded her to do as he said, and in such a tone that she dared not disobey.

She struck the blow tremblingly, hitting the red deer's tail that he wore, when lo! each half of his body took form, and instead of one handsome young warrior, there were two who were so much alike that one could not be distinguished from the other.

128

The One-Two, as they called themselves, went out to meet the people who were now advancing through the forest. The number of them was so great that it was a day's march from the foremost men to those at the end of the trail.

Their way went through a barren place, and they traveled all day without seeing trees or water. The next morning they began to grumble, for they suffered from thirst. As the day wore on they grumbled more and more and began to threaten the One-Two, though no one had been compelled to follow.

The Rattlesnake, who had much wisdom, said, "One-Two, now is the time to bring out your magic cup."

This cup was a large bowl of polished basswood. It could be held in the hand, and yet when one looked inside it one could not see the bottom. One-Two had received it from a magician when he first set out on his journey. He had sealed it as he had been told, with a water lily leaf and the balsam of the fir, and kept it to use when in great distress.

The brothers consulted together and decided to take the Rattlesnake's advice. They handed the cup from one to another. As soon as one had taken all that he wanted, even to what might have been half that it held, the cup was full again. But before it could be passed to the Wolf he was dead.

Then the people grumbled again, for the Wolf was brave and gave them courage. The brothers paid no attention to

129

the complaints, but one held the cup while the other took some water from it and with it he sprinkled the Wolf.

Wolf arose and cried: "Why did you disturb me? I was having such pleasant dreams."

They gave him the cup and he drank all that there was in it, but when he handed it to the brothers it did not refill.

They had brought but little food with them, and no animals crossed their path in the barren place; so they were hungry, and on the third day began again to grumble and to accuse the brothers.

The One-Two said nothing, but toward evening they said to the Wolf, who was keen of sight and of scent, "Is not that an antelope in the distance?"

"Yes," said the Wolf, "but it is the goat with many eyes, the watchman of Stone Shirt. Nevertheless I will go and kill it."

Then the Rattlesnake said, "Let me go, for the antelope will see you and will run away."

But the One-Two sent the Wolf, for they knew him to be the braver. He started at once, going in and out so as to hide in the bushes.

After he had gone, the Rattlesnake said to the brothers, "Do you see me?"

"No," was the answer, and they began to search for him. They looked in vain till the Rattlesnake chose to show himself, although they were standing in an open space where there was no place to hide.

The Rattlesnake again asked to be allowed to hunt the antelope. The brothers told him he might go, and in a few hours he returned with the game on his shoulders.

The Wolf saw him as he passed, and at first was very angry, but afterward he said to himself, "What does it matter, so long as the people get food?"

Again they were without water. The One-Two changed themselves into doves, took the magic cup and flew with it toward the lodge of Stone Shirt, which they knew was on the edge of a lake.

The daughters of Stone Shirt bathed in the lake every morning, and having been annoyed by birds peeping at them from the bushes, they set a snare for them.

The One-Two, knowing nothing of this, were caught, and the maidens carried them to a lodge. Stone Shirt looked at them with suspicion, for he knew no such birds lived thereabouts, and he feared they were spies. His daughters, however, persuaded him not to kill them. They stroked them and fed them and in the morning let them fly away.

The brothers went back to the bushes where they had dropped the cup, filled it, and flew with it to their camp.

The next day they ventured near Stone Shirt's lodge in their natural form. This time they saw their mother. She did not believe their story at first, for she had left only one child. But when they explained how everything had happened, she begged them not to fight Stone Shirt, and told them about his armor and his daughters' arrows.

131

But they could not be persuaded. They told her they would surely fight the giant the next day, and warned her not to go down to the lake for fear she might be hit by a stray arrow.

That night the One-Two disguised themselves as mice and crept into the wigwam of Stone Shirt, where they nibbled the strings of all his bows. The Rattlesnake went with them and hid himself behind a rock on which Stone Shirt sat every morning.

When the giant appeared as usual, the Rattlesnake bit him. He leaped high in the air and exclaimed. "We are betrayed!"

His daughters seized their bows and arrows, but found them useless, as the strings had been gnawed.

The cry of Stone Shirt had roused the warriors who, having advanced in the night, were lying in ambush near his lodge. They let fly a shower of arrows and then rushed from their hiding place.

Both the maidens were struck, and waving their hands to their enemies to fall back, they sang a death song and fell dead across the path that led to the lodge.

One-Two were very sorry, for the maidens had been kind to them. They buried them with great mourning, but the bones of Stone Shirt were left to rot as he had left those of their father, the Crane.

The Great
Wizard

Tangled Hair, son of the West Wind, was a giant in size
and his face was as black as the feathers of the crow. His
hair was of twisted snakes, gray, black, and spotted, with
an adder raising its copper-colored head for his crown,
while a rattlesnake spread itself across his shoulders. He
was the greatest of all wizards, and could change himself
into any bird or beast at will, could disguise his voice, and
did both good and evil as he felt inclined.

He lived with his grandmother, who had been thrown
from the moon by a jealous rival. Their lodge was on the
edge of the prairie not far from the Big Sea Water.

He himself did not know his power until one day while
playing with a beautiful snake, whose colors were brighter
than any of those upon his head, he found that by means

of it he could do magic. He had caught the snake and kept it in a bowl of water, feeding it every day on birds and insects. By chance he let fall some seeds, which were turned into birds as they touched the water, and the snake greedily devoured them. Then he discovered that everything he put into the water became alive.

He went to the swamp where he had caught the snake, for others, which he put into the bowl. Happening to rub his eyes while his fingers were still wet he was surprised to find how much clearer things at a distance appeared.

He gathered some roots, powdered them, and put them into the water. Then he took a little of the water into his mouth and blew it out in spray which made a bright light. When he put the water on his eyes he could see in the dark. By bathing his body with it he could pass through narrow or slippery places. A feather dipped into it would shoot any bird at which it was aimed, and would enter its body like an arrow.

He was able to heal wounds and sicknesses and to conquer all his enemies, but for all this he was a bad spirit nearly all his life.

His father, the West Wind, had entrusted Tangled Hair's brothers with the care of three-fourths of the earth, the north, the south, and the east, but gave nothing to him, the youngest. When he was old enough to know how he had been slighted, he was very angry and sought to fight his father.

134

He took his bearskin mittens and dipped them into the snake water, thereby making them strong with magic, so that he could break off great boulders by merely striking them. He chased his father across the mountains, hurling boulder after boulder at him until he drove him to the very edge of the earth. He would have killed the West Wind if he had dared, but he was afraid of his brothers, who were friendly to one another, and he knew that he could not stand against the three. So he compelled his father to give him power over serpents, beasts, and monsters of all kinds, and to promise him a place in his own kingdom after he should have rid the earth of them.

Having thus secured his share, he returned to his lodge, where he was sick for a long time from the wounds that he had received.

One of his first adventures after he had recovered was capturing a great fish, from which he took so much oil that when he poured it into a hollow in the woods, it formed a small lake, to which he invited all the animals for a feast.

As fast as they arrived he told them to jump in and drink. The bear went in first, followed by the deer and the opossum. The moose and the buffalo were late and did not get as much as the others. The partridge looked on until nearly all the oil was gone, while the hare and the marten were so long in coming that they did not get any. That is why animals differ so much in fatness.

When they had done feasting, Tangled Hair took up

136

his drum, beat upon it, and invited his guests to dance. He told them to pass around him in a circle, keeping their eyes shut all the time.

When he saw a fat fowl pass by him he wrung its neck, beating loudly on his drum to drown its cries and the noise of its fluttering. After killing each one, he would call out, "That's the way, my brothers. *That's* the way!"

At last a small duck, being suspicious of him, opened one eye, and seeing what he was doing, called as loudly as she could, "Tangled Hair is killing us," and jumped and flew toward the water.

Tangled Hair followed her, and just as she was getting into the water, gave her a kick which flattened her back, and straightened her legs out backward, so that she can no longer walk on land, and her tail-feathers are few to this day.

The other birds took advantage of the confusion to fly away, and the animals ran off in all directions.

After this Tangled Hair set out to travel, to see if there were any wizards greater than himself. He saw all the nations of red men, and was returning quite satisfied, when he met a great magician in the form of an old wolf, who was journeying with six young ones.

As soon as the wolf saw him, he told the whelps to keep out of the way, for Tangled Hair's fame for cruelty and wickedness had been carried everywhere by the animals and birds he had tried to kill.

As the young wolves were running off, Tangled Hair

said to them, "My grandchildren, where are you going?
Stop and I will go with you."

The old wolf was watching him and came up in time to
answer, "We are going to a place where we can find most
game, where we may pass the winter."

Tangled Hair said he would like to go with them and
asked the old wolf to change him into a wolf. Now this
was very foolish, for he thereby lost his power, whereas
if he had changed himself into one he might still have kept
it, but even the greatest wizard did not know everything.

The old wolf was only too glad to grant his wish, and
changed him into a wolf like himself. Tangled Hair was
not satisfied and asked to be made a little larger. The wolf
made him larger, and as he was still dissatisfied, he made
him twice as large as the others.

Tangled Hair was better pleased, but he still thought
he might be improved, so he said to the old wolf, "Do
please make my tail a little larger and more bushy."

The wolf did this, and Tangled Hair found a large tail
very heavy to drag about with him.

Presently they came to the bottom of a ravine up which
they rushed into the thick woods where they discovered
the track of a moose. The young wolves followed it, while
the old wolf and Tangled Hair walked on after them,
taking their time.

"Which do you think is the swiftest runner among my
whelps?" said the wolf.

"Why the foremost one, that takes such long leaps," said Tangled Hair.

The old wolf laughed sneeringly, "You are mistaken," he said, "he will soon tire out. The one who seems to be slowest will capture the game."

Shortly afterward they reached a place where one of the young wolves had dropped a small bundle.

"Pick it up," said the wolf to Tangled Hair.

"No," replied he, "what do I want with a dirty dog skin?"

The wolf took it up and it was turned into a beautiful robe.

"I will carry it now," said Tangled Hair.

"Oh, no," said the wolf, "I cannot trust you with a robe of pearls," and immediately the robe shone, for nothing could be seen but pearls.

They had gone about six arrow flights farther when they saw a broken tooth that one of the young wolves had dropped in biting at the moose as it passed.

"Tangled Hair," said the wolf, "one of the children has shot at the game. Pick up his arrow."

"No," he replied, "what do I want with a dirty dog's tooth?"

The old wolf took it up, and it became a beautiful silver arrow.

They found that the young wolves had killed a very fat moose. Tangled Hair was hungry, but the wolf charmed him so that he saw nothing but the bones picked bare. After a time the wolf gave him a heap of fresh ruddy meat cut, so it seemed to Tangled Hair, from the skeleton.

"How firm it is!" he exclaimed.

"Yes," answered the wolf, "*our* game always is. It is not a long tail that makes the best hunter."

Tangled Hair was a good hunter when he was not too lazy to undertake the chase. One day he went out and killed a large fat moose, but having lived well in the wolf's lodge he was not very hungry, and so turned the carcass from side to side, uncertain where to begin. He had learned to dread the ridicule of the wolves, who were always showing him how little he knew as a wolf, yet he could not change himself into a man again.

"If I begin at the head," he said, "they will say I ate it backwards. If I cut the side first, they will say I ate it sideways." He turned it round so that the hindquarter was in front of him. "If I begin here, they will say I ate it forwards." But he began to be hungry, so he said, "I will begin here, let them say what they will."

He cut a piece off the flank and was just about to put it into his mouth when he heard the branches of a large tree creaking. "Stop, stop," he said to the tree, for the sound annoyed him. The tree paid no attention to him, so he threw down his meat, exclaiming, "I cannot eat with such a noise about!"

He climbed the tree and was pulling at the branch which

140

by rubbing against another had caused the creaking, when it was suddenly blown toward him and his paw was caught so that he could not get it out. Pretty soon a pack of wolves came along and he called out to them, "Go away, go away!"

The chief of the wolves knew Tangled Hair's voice and said to the others, "Let us go on, for I am sure he has something there he does not want us to see."

They found the moose and began eating it. Tangled Hair could not get to them, so they finished the animal, leaving nothing but the bones. After they had gone a storm arose which blew the branches of the trees apart, and Tangled Hair was able to get out, but he had to go home hungry.

The next day the old wolf said to him, "My brother, I am going to leave you, for we cannot live together always."

"Let me have one of your children for my grandson," said Tangled Hair.

The old wolf left the one who was the best hunter, and also the lodge.

Tangled Hair was disenchanted after the wolves had gone, and when he assumed his natural shape, his power as a wizard came back. He was very fond of his grandson and took good care of him, giving much thought night and day to his welfare. One day he said to him, "My grandson, I dreamed of you last night, and I feel that trouble will come to you unless you will heed what I say. You must not cross the lake that lies in the thick woods. No matter what may be the need or how tired you may be, go around it, even though the ice looks strong and safe."

In the early spring when the ice was breaking up on the lakes and rivers, the little wolf came to the edge of the water late in the evening. He was tired and it was such a long way around. He stood and thought to himself, "My grandfather is too cautious about this lake," and he tried the ice with his foot, pressing his weight upon it. It seemed strong to him, so he ventured to cross. He had not gone half way, however, when it broke and he fell in, and was seized by the serpents whose lodge was under the water.

Tangled Hair guessed what had happened to him when night came and again the day and he did not return. He mourned many days first in his lodge, and then by a small brook that ran into the lake.

A bird that had been watching him said, "What are you doing here?"

"Nothing," said Tangled Hair, "but can you tell me who lives in this lake?"

"Yes," said the bird, "the Prince of Serpents lives here, and I am set by him to watch for the body of Tangled Hair's grandson, whom they killed three moons since. You are Tangled Hair, are you not?"

"No," was the answer, "why do you think he would wish to come here? Tell me about these serpents."

The bird pointed to a beautiful beach of white sand where he said the serpents came just after midday to bask in the sun. "You may know when they are coming," said he, "be-

142

cause all the ripples will disappear and the water will be smooth and still before they rise."

"Thank you," said Tangled Hair. "I am the wizard Tangled Hair. Do not fear me. Come and I will give you a reward."

The bird went to him and Tangled Hair placed a white medal round his neck, which the Kingfisher wears to this day. While putting it on he tried to wring the bird's neck. He did this for fear it might go to the serpents and tell them he was watching for them. It escaped him, however, with only the crown feathers ruffled.

He went to the beach of white sand and changing himself into an oak stump waited for the serpents. Before long the water became smooth as the lake of oil he himself had once made. Soon hundreds of serpents came crawling up onto the beach. The Prince was beautifully white, the others were red and yellow.

The Prince spoke to the others and said, "I never saw that black stump there before. It may be the wizard, Tangled Hair."

Then one of the largest serpents went to the stump and coiled itself round the top, pressing it very hard. The greatest pressure was on Tangled Hair's throat, and he was just ready to cry out when the serpent let go. Eight of the others did the same to him, but each let go just in time. They then coiled themselves up on the beach near their Prince, and after a long time fell asleep.

Tangled Hair was watching them closely, and when he

143

saw the last one breathing heavily in sleep, he took his bow and arrows and stepped cautiously about until he was near the Prince, whom he shot and wounded.

The serpents were aroused by his cry, and plunging into the water, they lashed the waves so that a great flood was raised and Tangled Hair was nearly drowned. He climbed into a tall tree, and when the water was up to his chin he looked about for some means of escape. He saw a loon and said to him, "Dive down, my brother, and bring up some earth so that I can make a new world."

The bird obeyed him, but came up lifeless. He next asked the muskrat to do him the service, and promised him if he succeeded, a chain of beautiful little lakes surrounded by rushes for his lodge in future. The muskrat dived down, but floated up senseless. Tangled Hair took the body and breathed into the nostrils, which restored the animal to life. It tried again and came up the second time senseless, but it had some earth in its paws.

Tangled Hair charmed the earth till it spread out into an island, and then into a new world. As he was walking upon it, he met an old woman, the mother of the Prince of Serpents, looking for herbs to cure her son. She had a pack of cedar cords on her back. In answer to his questions she said she intended it for a snare for Tangled Hair.

Having found out all he wished, Tangled Hair killed her, took off her skin, wrapped it about him, and placing the cedar cord on his back, went to her lodge.

144

There he saw the skin of his beloved grandson hanging in the doorway. This made him so angry that he could hardly keep up the disguise. He sat down outside the door and began weaving a snare of the cedar cord, rocking himself to and fro and sobbing like an old woman. Someone called to him to make less noise and to come and attend to the Prince.

He put down the snare, and wiping his eyes, went in, singing the songs the old woman had told him would cure her son.

No one suspected him, and he pretended to make ready to pull out the arrow which he found was not deeply embedded in the Prince's side. Instead of pulling it out he gave it a sudden thrust and killed the Prince, but he had used so much force that he burst the old woman's skin. The serpents hissed and he fled quickly from the place.

He took refuge with the badger, and with its help he threw a wall of earth against the opening of their lodge so that no one could get at him. They had another opening behind the rock, through which they could bring in food so that they could not be starved out by the serpents.

Tangled Hair soon grew tired of living underground, so he started to go out, and, as the badger stood in his way, and did not move quickly enough to please him, he kicked the poor animal and killed him.

He then ran back toward the serpent's lodge, and finding the dead body of the Prince, which the serpents in their haste to follow him had left unburied, he put the skin around him and went boldly up to the serpent tribe. They were so frightened that they fell into the lake and never again ventured forth.

After many years of wickedness, Tangled Hair repented, and traveled to the end of the earth, where he built himself a lodge, and tried, by good deeds, to rid himself of remembrances. But even there he was a terror to men and beasts.

Having shown, however, that he was really sorry for his misdeeds, his father, the West Wind, gave him a part of his kingdom. He went to live beyond the Rocky Mountains, and took the name of the Northwest Wind.

White Cloud's Visit
to the Sun Prince

ONCE UPON a time, when there were no large cities in the western world, all the land being forest or prairie, five young men set out to hunt. They took with them a boy named White Cloud. He was only ten years old, but he was a swift runner and his sight was keen, so there were many ways in which he was useful to them.

They started before daylight, and had traveled a long way when, on reaching the top of a high hill, the sun suddenly burst forth. The air was free from mist, and there being but few trees or tall bushes near, the brightness dazzled them as it had never done before, and they exclaimed, "How near it is!"

Then one of them said, "Let us go to it," and they all agreed. They did not wish to take White Cloud with them, but he insisted upon going. When they continued to refuse he threatened to tell their parents and the Chief, who would surely prevent them from undertaking such a journey. Finally they consented, and each went home to make preparations. They shot some birds and a red deer on the way so as not to arouse the suspicions of their friends.

Before they parted they agreed to get all the moccasins they could and a new suit of leather apiece, in case they should be gone a long time and might not be able to procure clothes.

White Cloud had most difficulty in getting these things, but after coaxing to no purpose, he burst out crying and said, "Don't you see I am not dressed like my companions? They all have new leggings." This plea was successful, and he was provided with a new outfit.

As the party went forth the next day they whispered mysteriously to one another, taking care that such phrases should be overheard as "a grand hunt," and "we'll see who brings home most game." They did this to deceive their friends.

Upon reaching the spot from which they had seen the sun so near on the previous day, they were surprised to find that it looked as far away as it did from their own village. They traveled day after day, but seemed to come no nearer. At last they encamped for a season and consulted with one another as to the direction in which they should go. White Cloud settled it by saying, "There is the place of light" (pointing toward the east), "if we keep on we must reach it some time."

So they journeyed toward the east. They crossed the prairie and entered a deep forest, where it was dark in the middle of the day. There the Prince of Rattlesnakes had his warriors gathered round him, but the eldest of the party wore a "medicine" of snakeskin, so he and his companions were allowed to go through the woods unharmed.

They went on day after day and night after night through forests that seemed to have no end. When the Morning Star painted her face, and when the beautiful red glowed in the west, when the Stormfool gathered his harvest, when the South Wind blew silver from the dandelion, they kept on, but came no nearer to their object.

Once they rested a long time to make snowshoes and more arrows. They built a lodge and hunted daily until they had a good store of dried meat, as much as they could carry, and again they went on their way.

After many moons they reached a river that was running swiftly toward the east. They kept close to it until it flowed between high hills. One of these they climbed and caught sight of something white between the trees. They hurried on and rested but little that night, for they thought surely the white line must be the path that leads to the splendid lodge of the sun.

Next morning they came suddenly in view of a large lake. No land was on any side of it except where they stood.

Some of them being thirsty, stooped to drink. As soon as they had tasted, they spat out the liquid, exclaiming, "*Salt water!*"

When the sun arose he seemed to lead forth out of the farthest waves. They looked with wonder, then they grew sad, for they were as far away as ever.

After smoking together in council, they resolved not to go back, but to walk around the great lake. They started toward the north, but had only gone a short distance when they came to a broad river flowing between mountains. Here they stayed the night. While seated around their fire, someone thought to ask whether any of them had dreamed of water.

After a long silence the eldest said, "I dreamt last night that we had come wrong, that we should have gone toward the south. But a little way beyond the place where we encamped yesterday is a river. There we shall see an island not far out in the lake. It will come to us and we are to go upon it, for it will carry us to the lodge of the sun."

The travelers were well pleased with the dream, and went back toward the south. A few hours' journey from their old camp brought them to a river. At first they saw no island, but as they walked they came to a rise of ground and the island appeared to them in the distance. As they looked, it seem to approach.

Some were frightened and wanted to go away, but the courage of White Cloud shamed them, and they waited to

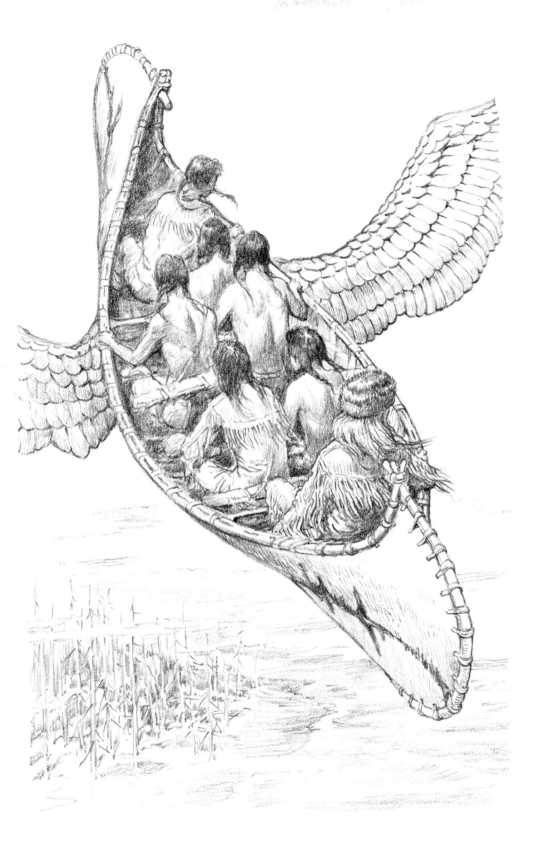

see what would happen. They saw three bare trees on the island, such as pine trees that have been robbed of their leaves by fire. As they looked, lo! a canoe with wings that flapped like those of a loon when it flies low down to the lake left the island.

It came swiftly over the water, and when it touched the land, a man with a white face and a hat on, stepped upon the shore and spoke to them, but they could not understand what he said. He motioned to them to mount the bird canoe, which they did, and were carried to the island.

There was a horrible noise and rattle like that made by the magician when he conjures the evil spirit from a sick man, then white wings sprang from the bare tree trunks, and they felt themselves moving over the water, as the deer bounds across the trail in the forest.

The night came and they saw the familiar stars above them, so they lay down to sleep, fearing nothing.

When the day dawned, they could see no shore anywhere, only the water of the lake. The Palefaces were kind, and gave them food and drink, and taught them words, such as they said to one another.

One moon had passed and another had come and nearly gone, when the Paleface Chief said they would soon find the shore, and he would take them to his Prince, who would direct them to their journey's end.

The Prince lived in a beautiful lodge of white stone. The walls were of silver, hung with silver shields and arrows.

152

His throne was of white horn carved with many figures. His robe was ermine, and he had many sparkling stones in his headdress.

He talked to White Cloud and listened to the story of their wanderings, their dreams and their disappointments, and spoke gently, trying to persuade them to give up their purpose. "See," said he, "here are hunting grounds, and fat deer, and game and fish enough for you, and none shall make war or trouble you. Why go farther?"

But they would not say. Whereupon the Prince proved himself a magician, for he told them in what direction they should go, and what would befall them. At the last they would come to the wigwam of the great wizard, Tangled Hair. They would hear his dreadful rattle three days before they reached his lodge, and the wizard would do his best to destroy them.

The Prince tried again to keep them, but as they would not stay, he gave them presents of food and clothing, and his warriors led them to the end of his country.

They went through many forests, but the trees were strange to them. They saw flowers springing in their path and vines upon the rocks and about the trees, but none were those they knew. Even the birds were strange, and talked in voices which they could not understand. But all this made them believe they were getting nearer to the Sun Prince.

After many moons the clothing which the Prince of the

153

Palefaces had given was worn out, so they put on their leather dresses again. Hardly had they done this, when they heard a fierce rattle and knew that they were near the wigwam of the wizard. The noise was dreadful and seemed to come from the center of the earth.

They had traveled far that day. The ground had been rough and stony and in many places covered with water through which they had been obliged to wade. They lighted a fire and sat down to dry their clothes and to rest. The noise of the rattle continued and increased so much that they broke up their camp and went toward the place which they knew must be Tangled Hair's lodge.

It was not a wigwam, but a lodge with many fireplaces, and it had eyes which glared like their campfire. Two of the travelers wished to go back or to try to get around the lodge, but White Cloud said, "Let the wizard see we are no cowards." So they went up to the door.

There they were met by Tangled Hair himself, who said, "Welcome, my grandsons!"

When they were seated in his lodge, he gave each some smoking mixture, and as they sat and smoked he said that he knew their history, and had seen them when they left their village. He took the trouble to do this so that they might believe what he was about to say.

"I do not know that all of you will reach your journey's end, though you have gone three-fourths of the way and are very near the edge of the earth. When you reach that place you will see a chasm below you and will be deafened by the noise of the sky descending upon the world. It keeps moving up and down. You must watch, and when it lifts you will see a little space. You must leap through this, fearing nothing, and you will find yourselves on a beautiful plain."

The wizard then told them who he was and that they had no need to fear him if they were brave men. He was not permitted to help weak men and cowards.

When the first arrow of daylight came into the lodge, the young men started up and refused to rest longer, so Tangled Hair showed them the direction they were to take in going to the edge of the world. Before they left he pointed out a lodge in the shape of an egg standing upon its larger end and said, "Ask for what you want and he who lives in that lodge will give it to you."

The first two asked that they might live forever and never be in want. The third and fourth asked to live longer than many others and always to be successful in war. White Cloud spoke for his favorite companion and for himself. Their wish was to live as long as other braves and to have success in hunting that they might provide for their parents and relatives.

The wizard smiled upon them and a voice from the pointed lodge said, "Your wishes shall be granted."

They were anxious to be gone, more especially when they found that they had been in Tangled Hair's lodge not a day, as they had supposed, but a year.

"Stop," cried Tangled Hair, as they prepared to depart,

"you who wished to live forever shall have that wish granted now." Thereupon he turned one of them into a cedar tree and the other into a gray rock.

"Now," said he to the others, "you may go."

They went on their way trembling, and said to one another, "We were fortunate to get away at all, for the Prince told us he was an evil spirit."

They had not gone far when they heard the beating of the sky. As they went nearer and nearer to the edge it grew deafening, and strong gusts of wind blew them off their feet. When they reached the very edge everything was dark, for the sky had settled down, but it soon lifted and the sun passed but a short distance above their heads.

It was some time before they could get courage enough to jump through the space. White Cloud and his friend at last gave a great leap and landed on the plain of which they had been told.

"Leap, leap quickly," called White Cloud to the others, "the sky is on its way down."

They reached out timidly with their hands, but just then the sky came down with terrific force and hurled them into the chasm. There they found themselves changed into monstrous serpents which no man could kill, so their wish was granted.

Meanwhile, White Cloud and his companion found themselves in a beautiful country lighted by the moon. As they walked on all weariness left them and they felt as if

156

they had wings. They saw a hill not far off and started to climb it, that they might look abroad over the country.

When they reached it, a little old woman met them. She had a white face and white hair, but her eyes were soft and dark and bright in spite of her great age.

She spoke kindly and told them that she was the Princess of the Moon, that they were now halfway to the lodge of her brother, the Sun Prince. She led them up a steep hill which sloped on the other side directly to the lodge of the Sun.

The Moon Princess introduced them to her brother, who wore a robe of a rich, golden color, and shining as if it had points of silver all over it. He took down from the wall a splendid pipe and a pouch of smoking mixture, which he handed to them.

He put many questions to them about their country and their people, and asked them why they had undertaken this journey. They told him all he wished to know, and in return asked him to favor their nation, to shine upon their corn and make it grow and to light their way in the forest.

The Prince promised to do all these things, and was much pleased because they had asked for favors for their friends rather than for themselves.

"Come with me," he said, "and I will show you much that you could not see elsewhere."

Before starting he took down from his walls arrows tipped with silver and with gold, and placed them in a

157

golden quiver. Then they set out on their journey through the sky.

Their path lay across a broad plain covered with many brilliant flowers. These were half hidden many times by the long grass, the scent of which was as fragrant as the flowers it hid. They passed tall trees with wide spreading branches and thick foliage. The most luxuriant were on the banks of a river as clear as crystal stone, or on the edge of little lakes which in their stony trails looked like bowls of water set there for the use of a mighty giant. Tribes of water fowl flew about, and birds of bright plumage darted through the forest like a shower of arrows. They saw some long, low lodges with cages filled with singing birds hanging on the walls, but the people were away.

When they had traveled half across the sky, they came to a place where there were fine, soft mats, which the young men discovered were white clouds. There they sat down, and the Sun Prince began making preparations for dinner.

At this place there was a hole in the sky, and they could look down upon the earth. They could see all its hills, plains, rivers, lakes, trees, and the big salt lake they had crossed.

While they were looking at a tribe of Indians dancing, something bright flew past them, downward through the hole in the sky and struck the merriest dancer of them all, a young boy, son of a great chief.

The warriors of his tribe ran to him and raised him with

great cries and sounds of sorrow. A wizard spoke and told them to offer a white dog to the Sun Prince.

The animal was brought, and the master of the feast held the choicest portion above his head, saying: "We send this to thee, Great Spirit," and immediately the roasted animal was drawn upward and passed through the sky. Then the boy recovered and went on dancing.

After White Cloud and his companion had feasted with the Sun Prince, they walked on till they saw before them a long slope that was like a river of gold, flowing across silver sands.

"Keep close to me," said the Sun Prince, "and have no fear. You will reach your home in safety."

So they took hold of his belt, one on either side of him, and felt themselves lowered as if by ropes. Then they fell asleep.

When they awoke they found themselves in their own country, and their friends and relatives were standing near them, rejoicing over their return. They related all their adventures, and lived many years in honor and in plenty, the Sun Prince smiling upon them in all their undertakings.

About the Illustrator

LORENCE F. BJORKLUND grew up in St. Paul, Minnesota. After apprenticeship to a mural painter, work in sculpture, and lessons in drawing from his father, he won a scholarship to Pratt Institute in Brooklyn. He has illustrated numerous books, both adult and juvenile titles, many of them having to do with the American Indians and the West which he knows so well. In addition to his own book, FACES OF THE FRONTIER, which presents his drawings and impressions of American frontier life, he and his daughter, Karna, collaborated on THE INDIANS OF NORTHEASTERN AMERICA.

Today, Lorence Bjorklund and his wife live in Croton Falls, New York. Summers are spent in South Thomaston, Maine, on Penobscot Bay.

Leisure time hobbies include building models, making replicas of firearms of the Middle Ages, rebuilding precision metal-working tools, lapidary work, and wood carving. But, as always, drawing is Lorence Bjorklund's first love.